I0667865

based on a true story

Two gay couples meet at an idyllic mountain cabin to celebrate Thanksgiving. As the four men reminisce of their college years, coming out, and recall their past friends and former lovers, a shocking and fatal tale of obsession unfolds.

Praise for the writings of Jameson Currier

"Currier is adept at drawing a fine line between the erotic and the tragic, and at telling stories that 'although personal, are also the stories of our community.'"
—*The New York Times Book Review*

"A writer who consistently surprises and delights, Currier's dynamism will surely carry his literary career to higher heights."
—*Bay Area Reporter*

"The breadth of Currier's personal experience is evident in his writing, which is moving without resorting to melodrama, familiar without feeling clichéd."
—*Windy City Times*

"As a writer, Currier should be lauded for his creative decision to avoid the all-too-common formulaic trappings of most current novels written for and about gay men."
—*Lambda Literary*

"Jameson Currier's kind of fiction can recreate reality more accurately than a cinema verité account of our daily lives."
—*The Washington Post Book World*

Also by Jameson Currier

based on a true story

a novel by

JAMESON CURRIER

Chelsea Station Editions

New York

Cover art by Duane Hosein
Book design by Peachboy Distillery & Designs

Published by Chelsea Station Editions
362 West 36th Street, Suite 2R
New York, NY 10018
www.chelseastationeditions.com
info@chelseastationeditions.com

Paperback ISBN: 978-1-937627-04-1
Ebook ISBN: 978-1-937627-38-6
Library of Congress Control Number: 2015950683

First Edition

based on a true story

To those who survived,
and in memory of those
not so fortunate.

So much of a novelist's writing, as I have said, takes place in the unconscious: in those depths the last word is written before the first word appears on paper. We remember the details of our story, we do not invent them.
Graham Greene, *The End of the Affair*

ONE

On the afternoon Scott and Aiden arrived, we sat outside rocking in the porch chairs in the thin, cold air. The view was magnificent that day, in spite of the fact that three days before heavy rain and winds had toppled the last of the bright autumn foliage from the branches. The sky was a flat baby blue, the mountains around us bare and brown, the ground black and soggy with decaying leaves, the dark evergreens clustered in the valley below and clinging to the slopes above us like patches of damp moss found on exposed river stones. Harley joined us after he had finished splitting the last logs and carried the bundles of firewood we would use during the following days to a bin beside the hearth in the Great Room; Zero, our amber-coated, over-enthusiastic mix of a collie and German shepherd, followed beside him, barking out a friendly, but loud, welcome to our visitors.

I had tried not to appear too disordered in the chaos of the house when I had given them a quick tour of the cabin, helping Scott carry their knapsacks, suitcases, and plastic shopping bags to the guest bedroom I had cleaned of Harley's clutter. Now, Scott and Aiden stood politely together on the deck while I chattered on about the enhancements we had made since purchasing the A-framed cabin six months ago, while Zero sniffed at our guests' pants legs, panting and barking to be recognized. Harley nodded and smiled at my glorification of our rustic retreat, adding only a few low-key, no-nonsense comments to my overly-enthusiastic descriptions of our home improvement schemes, such as "the wiring was no good" and "the shingles were rotted away," while trying to keep Zero's enthusiasm restrained. Scott and Aiden were winded from their two-day stay in Atlanta and the three-hour drive north this morning had left them sluggish; Scott had suggested that a brisk outdoor respite might help revive them and, while Harley described the repairs he had made to the dining table we had found at a flea market, I left them to go inside to the kitchen and make a pot of coffee for Aiden, a die-hard city boy who did not seem to be enamored of Scott's suggestion to linger outdoors and was scowling at Zero's inability to settle down and be quiet.

I was a bit unnerved to leave them all alone so quickly, feeling that it was my obligation to make sure they were at ease with each other and Zero not too much of a pest. I had not met Aiden, Scott's lover for the past two years, until this day; Harley, my boyfriend and housemate for the last half-a-year, had not met either of our guests until he stepped up onto the porch toting the logs in his arms, and I had considered the awkwardness all of us might feel before I had extended an invitation to the couple to visit us for the Thanksgiving holidays. Harley could come off as a bit intimidating; a big bear of a man in his late forties, he was six feet tall, balding and sporting a devilish grin surrounded by a bristly gray goatee and he had an assortment of tattoos which at any time as he moved about doing his various household projects could be seen peeking out beneath his flannel sleeves and neck collars. We had been introduced by a mutual friend more than two years before at a bar in Asheville where older gay men often hooked up in an awkward and suspicious manner, but Harley had been drunk and obnoxious that night, trying to pick a fight with me by saying he could beat me at pool with one hand tied behind his back (and which he could, since I was a lousy player, having only a dim impression of how the game was played). I refused the challenge and a few nasty remarks were exchanged between us and I left the bar quickly, since Harley easily outsized me and was looking to get into trouble. A year later he was re-introduced to me via the same friend, but this time Harley was sober, repentant, openly gay, and a changed man, "trying to sort out the mess of my life," he explained to me, since he was closing in tighter to that half-century marker (just as I was). I'd always believed we were a strange match, I was more city than country and Harley was just the opposite; our relationship had become a balancing act of compromises, one of which was my determination to find contentment and relaxation at the house we now co-inhabited, since I considered myself on the upside of a potential retirement. Harley's home improvement projects were ways of keeping himself occupied and sober, and Zero, in fact, had turned out to be a godsend by demanding his constant attention and affection. I could never keep up with Harley's own restless energy even at my most sane moments, and I often opted out of many of his more long-winded schemes, preferring instead to turn into a vegetable for a few hours, watching TV or reading a book or, at my best, cooking up something simple on the vintage 1950s double porthole stove we had inherited with the house.

Scott and I were more similar in physique and temperament, though the years and aging had made Scott my thinner and classier alter-ego, his thick head of hair now fully gray and neatly styled, whereas my own was a bit ragged and always seemed to be needing a trim. Scott was dressed that afternoon just as I had met many him twenty-seven years before; conservative in his button-down shirt, khaki pants, and loafers, his sweater was more expensive than one of my mortgage payments. We had met at a cocktail party in Manhattan in the months after we had both graduated college and moved to the city as eager and adventurous young men and, after a short, romantic dalliance with each other, we soon became better friends than lovers, kindred expatriates of unaccepting Southern families rather than committed significant others. Scott, who had arrived to

Manhattan from Mobile, Alabama, was working as a theater critic for a downtown weekly tabloid when we first met and I was an aspiring actor. I often went with him to see plays or musicals in tiny theaters in the most unlikeliest of places in the city, the "sludge at the bottom of the cup," was how he often described those shows. Scott maintained high standards for these "shoe-box presentations" and was easily disappointed by what he watched. Myself, a starry-eyed north Georgia boy, I had quickly given up my dream of making it on Broadway (or even off-) once I had bumped up again the limitless competition and found both discouragement and the recognition that I had no real acting, dancing or singing talent, though I never gave up my love of watching live performances, singing show tunes, and following the gossip of celebrity-driven drama. By day I worked at a succession of temporary jobs in the months that I was new to the city—telephone answerer, legal proofreader, dog walker, bike messenger, until I landed a permanent position as a copy editor at an advertising agency, where I stayed for many years until my own exit from Manhattan. I patiently worked my way up the cut-throat, backstabbing corporate ladder, one stressful account at a time, until I was at an obscenely high-paid management level. Scott migrated to California in the early 1990s, burned out by deaths of so many of his lovers and friends from AIDS and finished with his own desperate and despondent activism, but suspiciously hopeful that the newly-elected Democratic administration that arrived with the Clinton presidency would bring about a more optimistic moment for the gay community. On the West Coast, he worked his way up from a stringer of a Hollywood trade publication to its editor-in-chief, then abandoned the publication to edit a glossy lifestyle monthly which relied more on photographs and graphics than it did on journalistic content. Aiden was one of Scott's art designers—a younger, softer, more narcissistic version of Scott.

Scott's first commitment for the Thanksgiving holidays was to spend time with his mother in Mobile, an effort he had said would require "a minimum of three or four hours before her chattering drives me crazy." From Alabama, he and Aiden had driven north in a rented car to the outskirts of Atlanta to spend time with Aiden's sister Michelle and her family, and Scott had warned me in an e-mail that Aiden's sister's histrionics might even make a weekend visit with us impossible. (My own parents had left their suburban north Georgia home where they had raised their four children to retire to sunny southern Florida and I and my older brother and two younger sisters no longer had any connections with our past in East Marietta, now a sprawling and ever-expanding fundamentally conservative suburb in Cobb County on the outskirts of Atlanta; instead, we had become a scattered clan with outposts in La Jolla, California; Lake Charles, Louisiana; and Wheeling, West Virginia. I seldom traveled any more to see my siblings and their spouses and children, telling them that they could find me at our parents' home during my winter holidays if they cared to see me.) But Scott had also written that he was likely to be the trump card in Aiden's family drama, and that Michelle's conservative "good 'ole boy" husband never felt comfortable with a too-trendy West Coast gay couple around their small suburban house, and that an early departure could even be more likely, which was exactly how it had transpired when Scott reached me on his cell phone that morning and said they were leaving Atlanta within the hour.

Aiden, now in his early forties and the youngest of the four of us that holiday, had escaped the front porch and the cold air and found me in the kitchen as I was pouring the coffee into a mug for him, the air warm and heavy of hazelnut from the brew I had used. I asked him if he wanted sugar or another sweetener and he asked for a substitute for the real thing, his voice nasal and affected.

I did my best to show that I did not immediately dislike him because he was a younger and, in my opinion, a somewhat pretentious man, and I found the sweetener and asked if he preferred cream or low-fat milk. I knew his response before he even uttered it—the low-fat alternative—and I handed him the finished product and began making a cup for myself.

"I despise the cold," Aiden said, sipping at the coffee. "L.A. has made my blood so thin."

"Were you born in California?" I asked him.

"Goodness, no," he answered with a light, nervous giggle at the back of his throat. "Melville, Long Island. I used to play hooky all the time and take the train to Times Square. I just wanted to live someplace more exotic and tropical. L.A. was as far as I got."

I nodded and smiled, easily imagining Aiden in a floral shirt with a light sheen of perspiration on his brow, his eyes shaded by dark sunglasses and a large, fruity cocktail poised on top of his inflated stomach.

"Shall I spice it up for you?" I asked him, pointing toward his mug. "I've got some stuff hidden around here—brandy, rum, Grand Marnier—a housewarming gift from the realtor when we moved in."

"I don't dare," Aiden said, rolling his eyes. "Way too early in the day for me, even in this time zone. I'll only be soused and become stupid and useless. I still feel like I need to keep my wits about me."

I gave him a weak smile, which he ignored or, rather, did not notice because he was suddenly conscious of Inky lying by the kitchen door. Inky was a fifteen-year-old overfed black cocker spaniel that I had seen the day we had gone to adopt Zero from the ASPCA. Harley had taken immediately to Zero's friendliness and high-spirits, but I had been drawn to the lonely, lethargic puddle of black fur in another cage. Arthritic and near-blind, Inky had been given up to be "put down." His original owners had moved out of state some years ago and he had lived with a boy and his grandmother in Ednyville until the boy grew old enough to enlist in the Marines and the grandmother had died. The young soldier was stationed in Iraq and had no way of keeping care of the dog, so he brought him in after his grandmother's funeral hoping he might find a

14

home. But Inky seemed destined to be passed over for younger and more eager dogs and had long since passed through an acceptable period for the charity to shelter a dog, and in recent months he had developed vision problems with cataracts in his left eye. After the vet had reassured me that the dog was not in any kind of continual pain, I had arranged for a surgeon in Chapel Hill to remove the cataracts in Inky's left eye and then drove ten hours round-trip to pick him up and bring him home. Inky seldom moved from his spot by the kitchen door except for a brief morning walk to do his business, and I had trained him to sleep on a small rug that could be pushed or pulled to move him out of the way of any sort of kitchen traffic.

"You're not allergic, are you?" I asked Aiden.

"Heavens, no," he answered. "We have two dogs in LA. Nick and Nora. Jack Russell terriers that never settle down. I hated to have to leave them behind."

Aiden leaned down and petted Inky between the ears and asked how old he was, Inky responding with a thumping of his stub of a tail and Aiden complimenting the graying patterns of fur at his ears and chin.

"He doesn't like being too close to the stove," I said.

"The color must frighten him away," Aiden said and gave a nervous giggle. "Or are dogs color blind? I can never remember."

The bright red vintage stove was the house's oldest and oddest feature and I added my own nervous laugh in acknowledgment. Inside, I was cooking a fourteen-pound turkey which we would eat later that day (and use for left-overs for several days thereafter). Aiden opened the oven door and peered at the tinfoil-lined baking pan, the oil and juices cackling and popping as the heat rolled out and down to our feet.

"It'll be two hours or so before it's ready," I said. "If you're hungry, I could fix you something to tide you over. A sandwich?"

"I'm fine," he answered, which I knew meant he wasn't; I felt sure that Scott must be a difficult partner and that a visit with any kind of relatives, straight or otherwise, must have been strained. Gay men, myself included, have little patience when families and friends are less than tolerant at understanding the exasperation of our lives. I took the opportunity of the opened stove door, however, to baste the turkey some more.

"How is your sister doing?" I asked, thinking that if I brought the sore points to the surface that we might be able to wash our hands of them and continue with the weekend without looking back.

"She's a mess," he answered, "And she deserves to be one. I don't think I could go through what she has."

"I'm sure it's been a difficult process," I said. Aiden's eyes had only met mine once since our introduction, and that for the merest moment, and it seemed to me that they were skeptical and suspicious, not necessarily of me, but of some truth which he might reveal of himself. I did not know of Aiden's own romantic past. He had a handsome face with waifish features, tight, high cheekbones, a small, upturned nose, and long black eyelashes which seemed almost indecent on an adult man. That he loved Scott once—or still—I could only speculate on, but since he was eight years younger than the rest of us, I considered him as a member of another, younger generation. I did not know if he had personally experienced the changes the AIDS epidemic had so tragically and unexpectedly wrenched upon myself and Scott—we had both lost more lovers and friends than we wished to add up and it now felt like we carried ghostly baggage strapped to our backs, unable to talk about the epidemic we knew because it was not the epidemic that had continued.

With our mugs in hand, we moved from the kitchen to the Great Room, the wooden beams of the ceiling sloping up to a peak a floor above us. Harley and I had clustered our meager furnishings into a little dining area on one side of the room and a small sitting area around the oversized fireplace, but it

16

was the black, bear skin rug on the floor which Harley had purchased through a Web auction which had transformed all of our beaten second-hand furniture into something approaching rustic chic, even though its presence was often construed as politically incorrect by even our most conservative guests. I watched Aiden's eyes take in the gruesome expression still left on the snout of the grizzly thing and knew that it would provoke a remark—it always did from our first time visitors.

"Spooky," Aiden said. "Like the devil never left its face."

Then Aiden took a few steps toward the other side of the room where I had fashioned a nook of bookcases against the wall and angled a wooden schoolroom teacher's desk toward the window and the view of the mountains, a space I used more often than Harley did to pay bills, talk on the phone, or surf the Internet.

"Scott did say you had a lot of books," Aiden said, stepping a bit closer to the shelves and scanning the titles. They were mostly books I had read since my high school days, science fiction, fantasy, classic novels, as well as the gay-themed ones I had devoured in the late 1970s when I first moved to New York City. There were also shelves of history and self-help books, from gay life in the Roman Empire to finding a spiritual path as an agnostic. I was a book lover, treasuring a paperback of an Asimov novel I had read as a boy equally as much as I did a first edition of *The Great Gatsby*.

"I couldn't leave them behind when I left Manhattan," I said. "I gave away all my furniture, but the books felt like friends, so they came with me."

"Are you at work on something?" he asked, more out of politeness than from true interest. I was an accidental writer, not a trained one. During the most bleak period of my years in the New York—the mid-1980s—I had written a few short, episodic stories of my ex-boyfriends and ex-lovers—optimistic and dauntless young men like myself who had come to the city and had been caught up in the unfortunate drama of the first years of the AIDS epidemic. They were stories about expatriates, immigrants, random lovers, and my own transformation into an unexpected care partner. It was more therapeutic for me to do this than it was crafted storytelling, but after reading one of my tales at a friend's memorial service, an editor approached me about publishing it. So at about the same time that Scott left Manhattan for the sunny shores of the West Coast, I published an interlocking series of eulogies as a novel, a bittersweet accomplishment that I had never tried to reproduce or use to begin a new career because I considered it a realistic account and not a fictional one. They were all true stories, only the names of the dead had been changed. Kyle became Nate. Paul became Vince. Tony became Steve. I was only trying to come to grips with my inner confusions over the death of young men at a too early age. Friends who had read my novel told me that it was unbearably honest but so tragically sad it was hard to finish. I never expected my novel to become a best-seller (and which it didn't), and I never expected to become a full-time writer myself (and which I didn't). But everyone who knew of the book always asked if there was anything more or something else, as if they considered me busy at work on the next big project.

"I've been toying with a few ideas," I answered, though the truth was I hadn't written a stitch since I had left Manhattan two years before. The year that I had published my novel I had sat down to write a new one, but every one I attempted to write seemed too similar to my first effort, and the truth of the matter was I did not care to revisit the pain of those days or write that story again and I lost interest. There was a time when I tried to write other things—a science fiction story about life on another planet, a screenplay about an angel who falls to earth, but I was never that kind of creative writer or trained artist and so the inspiration to finish and publish those manuscripts never materialized. For a while I interviewed gay men who had been infected with the virus I had somehow avoided contracting myself, and then for a while I wrote about the political demonstrations I had attended and why I was still angry at both science and society. Writing was a healing process for me, a way to untangle the jumble of my mind, and once I had reached a certain acceptance—and maturation—it had just stopped. The need and ambition to continue to be a writer wasn't there. Over time I had learned it was easier to answer such a question as Aiden's by saying there was a next story waiting in the wings rather than disappointing my inquisitor or admitting that I had lost my youthful passion to write.

"Is this you?" Aiden asked next, picking up a framed photo that was on the desk. He had turned away from the books to the view through the window and the shadowy shapes that Harley and Scott and Zero's wagging tail cast on the outdoor planks of the porch deck when the pictures beside the computer monitor caught his attention. On the desk were mementos of my life before Harley and moving to the outskirts of Asheville. The photograph Aiden had picked up and studied a bit too closely had been taken in 1975 during my first visit to Asheville with my first boyfriend Jeff, taken by our friend Neal, who had driven us up from Atlanta to the mountains during spring break our sophomore year. I was nineteen years old that day, still more boy than young man, and though I had not admitted yet to anyone that I was gay and Jeff and I had not become sexually involved with each other, he was, at that moment Neal had snapped the photo, already the big love of my life.

"It's hard to imagine I was ever that skinny," I said, looking over Aiden's shoulder, feeling a pang of nostalgia furrow my forehead. "Or that young." Now it was my turn to give a nervous giggle. In the years since the photo had been taken exercise, stress, booze, and a series of unsuccessful diets had transformed me into an altogether different-looking man. It was even hard for me to recognize the blissful, optimistic youth I had once been.

Aiden hesitated with another picture of the younger me, recognizing in it a youngish Scott in the picture, but it went without comment and he placed the frame back on the desk and walked to the screen door. We stood and looked out at Scott and Harley talking on the porch. Scott brought a hand up to his lips and took a drag off the end of a cigarette. I swung the door open and said, "You still smoke?"

"Couldn't give it up," he answered.

"It's a nasty habit," Aiden said, with a bit too much venom in his voice. "At work, he has to go stand outside the building like all the other addicts."

"In the overall scheme of things, I'd say I've lost maybe ten years because of it," Scott said. "But it's kept me thin. My theory at least. It's my one vice."

"Flaw," Aiden said. "And not the only one."

"No, *luxury*, I think," Scott said, clearly trying to antagonize Aiden. "My little *luxury*, especially since the price went sky-high for a pack of these death sticks." In that moment I sensed that things were not well between the two of them and I wondered how we would all survive such close quarters for the rest of the weekend. I held the screen door open for Aiden as he walked outside, his coffee cup pressed against his chin as if he were waiting to blow across the surface. We stood silent as Scott finished his cigarette, more in awe of the expanse of nature around us, than of Scott's inhaling and exhaling. When old friends meet after many years, there is surprisingly little need for speech, and I had little to ask Scott except to know how he was really doing, where he thought things might go with Aiden, whose path with his boyfriend already seemed a rocky and difficult one. But Harley and Aiden were strangers, only circumstances had pulled them together, and there was no unspoken politeness to connect or shield them from each other.

"Tom has told me about your nephew Perry," Harley said to Aiden, holding Zero's eagerness at bay by patting his neck. "I hope your sister is handling it okay."

"*Hardly*," Aiden said, with every ounce of bitterness that coursed through his body.

I noticed that Aiden had failed to look at Harley when he had responded and I knew he must be uneasy with Harley's presence, but Aiden's posture and tone also seemed to me a condescending one, as if Harley were not hip enough—or upscale or young and pretty enough—to want to connect with and keep engaged in conversation. Harley worked for a towing company in Gastonia, about a half-hour's drive from the cabin, and even cleaned up and newly-shaved he displayed the rougher edges of a blue-collar worker. But Harley was also a smart and observant man, and he had a broad perspective about the mechanics of life that many of my other gay friends did not, and I knew him well enough now to know that he was aware of what Aiden thought of him, though Harley's response to it was to merely draw in a deep breath of the brisk mountain air and overlook it.

"It's an odd set of coincidences," Harley said. "Since Tom knew Neal so well."

"And odder because Scott met Neal years ago, too," I said.

"You knew Neal *before*?" Aiden said, his voice high and shrill, his eyes wide and suspicious. "Why didn't I know this?"

"I never realized it until Tom reminded me in an e-mail asking about Perry," Scott said, his eyes giving me a nervous flicker. "Almost a year-and-a-half after it was all over, but Tom had just heard about Neal. I didn't think it appropriate to bring up to you or your sister. It's no big secret. We all went to a party together one night. Neal was visiting Tom in New York."

Aiden's eyes were deflected into the bottom of his coffee mug, and I wished now I had spiked his drink with something, even without asking permission to do so. Aiden had a clear sense of drama, and of wanting to heighten it further, and perhaps a shot of booze could have made him mellower. "Do tell all," he said. "We're all ears. And we have plenty of time out here in the wilderness."

I cast my eyes toward Scott and it had seemed to me that he was frightened, not necessarily of me, or of what I would

21

say, but of some future consequence with Aiden. Harley cleared his throat and I knew he was about to leave, in search of some project to occupy himself rather than to witness the growing tension between our guests, but I placed my hand across his forearm, indicating it was best to stay while Zero cocked his ears back and looked between us. It was lucky, in a way, that a fourth person should be present for this story, given the situation's delicacy for Aiden.

"I knew Neal well," I said. "We met in college and were good friends. He came to New York to visit me a few years later. I think I was twenty-four. Maybe twenty-five at the time. It was Spring of 1981. May. Just before that horrendous article in the *Times* appeared. 'Rare Cancer Found in Homosexuals.'"

Scott laughed quietly. "It was an odd time for all of us," he said, sparing me of having to tell the tale. "We were so much younger."

"And wilder," I added. "Not so concerned about things."

"It must have made some kind of impression," Aiden said to Scott. "If you can recall it from all those years ago."

"That's just it," Scott said. "I do. And I don't. It was something that I simply forgot until Tom reminded me of it. Take a load off your feet, honey. I'll disclose all."

"Should we go inside?" I suggested, thinking this might potentially postpone Scott's tale, or at least the revelation of it, until sometime later, perhaps when Scott and Aiden were alone or in better moods.

"No, no, *no*," Aiden answered quickly. "Let's stay out here. The air is so clear here. Clear and inspiring."

So we took our seats in the rockers, three of us, at least. Harley sat on the porch railing, his back propped up against a column, the amphitheater of the valley and mountains behind him, Zero lying at the edge of his boot. Aiden sat his mug on the windowsill behind him and folded his arms across his chest, while Scott dug out a pebble that had worked its way into his loafer. He tossed it over the railing and then shifted his ankle up to rest against the opposite knee. "Well," he said, giving the word as much dramatic intonation as Aiden would, "this sort of build-up hardly compares with what follows."

TWO

I have always found it difficult to search through childhood experiences for clues to adult behavior. Why one child rebels while another restrains himself is as complex as why one gay man has no difficulty with expressing his sexuality and another may remain closeted for a lifetime. How my friend Neal arrived at college with a flawless self-confidence I can only speculate on and piece together from bits of information I knew of his years before the age of sixteen. He was always tall and large for his age, which must have given him an advantage over most of the other smart-mouth, mischievous boys at his high school. He was always intelligent and ahead-of-his class and he took his studying seriously, hence the partial scholarship to college he had earned.

Neal's self-confidence played a large part in determining my own in my college days. I was fraught with uncertainties at every step—whether to buy a car, take a linguistics course, or accept the invitation from a sorority girl to attend her prom. I could always count on Neal to give me a quick and thoughtful opinion. (No, on the car; yes, on linguistics class; and yes, on the sorority prom—the girl who had asked me would never even consider allowing me to "go all the way" with her even if I wanted to, so at worst, the evening would include a free meal and a couple of drinks.) My sophomore year, when I was cast as Hamlet in a college production of Tom Stoppard's play,

Rosencrantz and Guildenstern Are Dead simply because I had the right "troubled, young handsome look" and not an iota of talent, it was Neal who gave me pointers on how to walk across the stage, how to hold a prop, how to slow my diction so that I was thoughtfully speaking my lines and not regurgitating them from memory. How he knew this I never questioned; in my mind he was neither an actor nor a stage director in his past; he simply arrived with these instincts intact.

In the eye of my memory he arrived certain of his homosexuality, too—his first encounter with another man was at the request of a neighbor whose wife was away, dropping his shorts to his ankles and allowing the man to first examine his testicles, then arouse his cock and bring him to orgasm. He was fourteen years-old and the man was forty-two. By the time Neal left for college, he had given out blow jobs in the restroom of Sears, had anal intercourse as the active partner with a member of his high school basketball team, and had enticed the married neighbor to fuck him. I didn't learn this right away about him, of course; no, it was something like three-years into our college lives when he sat down on the rug in my apartment, lit a joint, and confessed this prior experience and knowledge of himself. At the time I was stupidly, boyishly, infatuatingly in love with my first boyfriend—our mutual friend Jeff. And it was Neal who offered me more advice when Jeff began breaking my heart, staying out with other men or abandoning me at a club because he thought another guy was "hot."

"Let's not leave Harley out in the cold," Scott said, glancing away from Aiden toward Harley and the panorama of mountains behind him. "I don't know how much Tom has told you about Neal, but he was a big guy like yourself. Thickly built. Intimidating. People didn't always remember him, however. The details of his face, his posture, what he said, that sort of thing. But they always noticed him because he was a large man. What I remember most about him is that he came to New York with an agenda." Scott turned to me and said, "Correct me if I'm wrong on this."

26

"He had a list of things that he wanted to do or places he wanted to see while he was in town," I added.

"It wasn't a written list," Scott continued. "But it was certainly one that a gay man would have acquired over the course of time of studying or reading about the city—things beyond the typical tourist destination. For instance, he wanted to see Studio 54, even though it was already passé. And go to The Saint, because even by then it was a legend. He wanted to go to a couple of bars downtown. This was in the early 1980s, you know, Christopher Street was hopping with guys at all hours, and there was always something going on, men parading back and forth, east to west, Badlands at the end, Sheridan Square at the center. He wanted to see Julius's, too, which was sort of an odd choice, considering it was one the more sedate gay places on his list. He wanted to go to the St. Mark's Baths. And the porn theater on Union Square. But he wanted to see other places, not just gay stuff. Soho and Chinatown. The Dakota, because this was not long after John Lennon was shot. He wanted to go to Bloomingdale's, Tiffany's, and the Guggenheim. And MoMA and the Met."

"He'd never been to the city before," I added. "And after we graduated I hadn't kept in touch with him, but he had tracked me down through the Alumni Office because he had read that I was living in New York and working for an advertising firm. So he called me and asked if he could come up for a visit. I hadn't turned into the kind of New Yorker yet who would say no to a request like that. I still had plenty of college friends visiting me then. I was even putting up friends of friends, letting them crash in a sleeping bag on my floor or sleep on this thing I used to have that mimicked being a couch—a sort of captain's bed with a huge Styrofoam pillow at the back which you could just lift off in one giant piece. So it never occurred to me to say no to him, either, because I was happy to have company. I didn't have a lot of good, close friends in town. Scott was one of the few guys who I knew well."

"I had been invited to a roof-top party on the Upper West Side that Saturday," Scott continued. "It was close to Memorial Day, I think. I asked Tom to come with me and he said he had a houseguest and I told him to bring him along."

"But I asked Scott what he was doing the rest of the day and if he wanted to join me and Neal," I said. "I had gotten free passes to the Met through a business acquaintance who worked in the *Times* advertising department and I asked if Scott wanted to come along with us."

"I love the Met," Scott said. "All that Egyptian stuff was in vogue. King Tut had just finished making a splash. They had finished building the new wing for the Temple of Dendur. So I said yes, because I hadn't seen that part of the museum yet. And the plan was that we would get something to eat afterward and then go to the party."

"I met them on the steps at the entrance—that rising plateau of stairs along Fifth Avenue. From the top I could see Tom walking uptown and the guy who was with him, so I had a chance to study them as they got closer. He was about twice TomTom's size. A big guy. Sort of non-descript after that. He didn't have a handsome face, but he wasn't ugly. Sort of blondish-brown hair. Pale skin. I thought he looked like a big dough boy. It was summer and he looked like he hadn't ever been out in the sun."

"I got a dose of his temperament right up front, though," Scott continued. "When we went inside he was insistent on seeing the Greek statues before we went to the Temple. And there was no point in arguing with him. He was stubborn. Almost to the point of throwing a fit. After the Temple, he wanted to see some pre-Columbian stuff that was just hard to find in the museum and he was clearly pissed that we didn't know exactly where they were."

"There was a bit of a disagreement over dinner, too," I said. "Scott suggested we walk through the park and eat at a diner on the West Side before going to the party. Neal wanted to eat at this café in the Village that was supposed to be hip and bohemian at the same time, and we tried to convince him that it was a bit of a schlep and that the food was expensive and lousy. But he said he would pay the cab fare, so off we went downtown."

"I don't remember talking to him about a lot of things," Scott said. "He was living in Dallas at the time. Was working as an accountant for some kind of grocery chain, I think. I asked him some things about the Dallas area but it was clear to me that he didn't like where he was and didn't want to talk about it. He talked about wanting to move back to Atlanta. His company had an office there. But what kind of guy he was? I don't know other than being slightly temperamental. I can tell you this, though—he was definitely gay. He had all the interests that any gay man would have—asking about what kind of guys went to this bar, what sort of scene went on at this club—that sort of thing." Scott glanced over to me and then asked, "He left the party early as I recall, didn't he?"

"He went to the Mineshaft," I answered. "A sex club I had never had the courage to go to, even in my raunchiest periods. I didn't see him till the following morning when he showed back up at my apartment. The rest of the trip was about the same. We would do things during the day or when I got off work. And he would end up at a sex club and show back up at my apartment the next morning. It's like he only used my place to shower and change clothes. But I had a lot of people do that while they were visiting me. I didn't think it that unusual. But he left me a memorable parting gift."

"How so?" Harley asked.

"He left during a work day. Tuesday or Wednesday morning, I think. I had given him keys, told him to lock the apartment door and slide the keys back underneath, through the crack. When I came home I found he had decorated the leaves of a large fern I had at the time next to my window. He had used ribbon to tie joints—pot—marijuana joints—to almost all the branches of the plant as a thank you gift. I think that stash must have lasted me almost two years. He never came back to the city after that. We kept in touch here and there—tried to at least. I had to remind Scott that he had met Neal."

"He didn't make that big of an impression on me. I was glad to forget him. So it never occurred to me that I should tell you the story," Scott said to Aiden.

Aiden's displeasure continued to register on his face, so Scott continued. "When we had dinner in Atlanta with Aiden's nephew, I thought his boyfriend looked familiar, but I couldn't really place him, so I just thought he must have reminded me of someone else. I've reached that strange age where *everyone* seems to remind me of someone else. I see other people's features in their faces. It didn't register to me that I might have already met him because he looked so different than the guy I had met in New York and we were in another city and so many years later. He was slimmer, in great shape, not an ounce of body fat on him, like he had served in the military for years. And Neal never let on that he had met *me* before."

Scott grinned and pushed a hand through his hair and looked at his lover and added, "I never mentioned it to you because I didn't find it worthwhile. I only told you that TomTom had known Neal years ago. When they were in school. But that was long after the fact."

"We lived on the same dormitory hall my first two years," I told Aiden. "That's how I met him. He changed roommates several times in the first few weeks until he ended up getting a private room on my hall. I don't think it was because he was difficult or anti-social—or I didn't think that at the time. He just saw that having a private room was of a sort of power status thing and Neal was into that stuff. Trying to look better than the other guys. None of the other guys ever talked about him, teased him, said any derogatory things about him, though—it wasn't like that. In fact, he was pretty un-memorable in college, too, if you weren't his friend. He went about his classes, got decent grades, never caused any scandals or trouble. But I know whenever I talked to him about somebody else, he seemed to know everything there was to know about this

30

person, or things that I didn't know, so it appeared that people were talking to him, confiding in him, like he knew everyone's dark, little secret."

"And yours?" Scott asked. "What was your dirty little secret?"

Scott's tone made Zero lift his head and give a nervous bark and we all laughed at the dog's perfect timing.

"Well, mine was neither dark nor dirty," I answered. "I did have an ongoing problem, which I was embarrassed to admit. I had a penchant for bouncing checks. I didn't know how to balance a checkbook—still don't—Harley will confirm that for you—I can't remember when I withdrew money or when I deposited money, so it just becomes a confusing tangle for me. Neal found that amusing. He knew that I had bounced my first tuition check. I don't know how he knew it, but he did. He was from a working class family in Valdosta and so he knew every cent he had and how he had earned it. He was meticulous about money right from the day I met him and he told me he owned a car that he parked off-campus. That was also another power point. Freshmen were not allowed to have cars. But you could get away with it if you kept it at an off-site lot. He drove us to a lot of places freshman year. He was happy to be a chauffeur because it made people dependent on him. And he could collect on a favor if he needed one himself—not that he did. As I recall, he never asked for help from anyone."

"We had a lot of mutual interests. Only we approached them differently. I think because we knew each other before we found out we liked some of the same things made us better friends. We both ended up in the Glee Club. And the student theater group. And working for the yearbook. But it began when there was a guy on our hall we both liked. This was before I came out, before I even accepted the basic truth of myself, and before I knew Neal was gay, too, so it wasn't like it was an overtly mutual sexual interest in the same guy—even though it was, subliminally—but more of an outward curiosity about him and the need to have friends because we were all lonely and adrift in the same big boat. New. Freshman. Trying to find our bearings. The guy's name was Jeff. And he lived in one of the rooms between mine and the one that ended up being Neal's private one. I should probably say that Jeff was one of the reasons why my friendship with Neal lasted as long as it did—well after graduation, in fact. Jeff was my first infatuation. First best friend. First boyfriend. First lover. Puppy love, gay-boy romance. However you want to describe it. The first guy I really fell head-over-heels for. We stayed friends until he died.

"Jeff was about my height. Wiry, thin build when I met him. Dark, curly hair but with the tips turning blond. He had a thick sideburns and a heavy black stubble that I found fascinating because I could go days without shaving myself and not even have any fuzz on my chin. I think that I had hardly even passed through puberty, so even though we were in the same class and were the same age, he seemed like a wiser, more-experienced older brother to me. And I had never had that kind of friendship before or even had a guy for a best friend. I was always a loner and bookish kid in high school. So when Jeff took an interest in having me as his friend, and sort of educating me in the ways of the world at the same time, I was both thankful and smitten. It didn't take long for me to learn that Jeff was openly out and gay. You have to remember. This was the early 70s. I knew nothing of that kind of behavior—I didn't even know what 'out' meant—I was naive and closeted about myself and my sexual feelings, other than recognizing that there were certain guys who aroused me and Jeff was one of them. Jeff was the first guy I kissed, the first guy I had sex with, the first guy I went to a gay club with, the first guy who broke my heart. But that's jumping way ahead to when we were juniors and living off campus together.

"At the beginning of freshman year Jeff was the person who suggested that I audition for the campus Glee Club. It was only a passing comment he made to me in the hallway one day when I was headed out to class—I'm not sure we had even formally introduced ourselves to each other. I nodded and said, maybe, not really giving it much attention, until Neal asked me the same question the next day. I ended up walking over to the music department with both of them the next night when they were having auditions—a sort of dormitory outing—and that was how our lives became entwined. I certainly couldn't sing and could barely read music. I went because of Jeff and Neal and I always think that was how I got into the group—they needed able and willing bodies who could look like they could carry a tune and I was one of them. The next afternoon I was talking with Neal in the hallway and he seemed to know everything about Jeff. That his father had been in the military, that he was from Maryland, that he was at school on a partial scholarship. Now I can see that this was one of the ways that Neal was manipulative with other people, and in a way with me, because he wanted to be my friend. Information is power—that sort of thing. But back then, these were details I was curious to know because I already had a big, subconscious crush on Jeff. I was attracted to him and struggling with how to handle that attraction and begin a friendship at the same time. Luckily, youth and immaturity keep us in denial about many things, even when it is so easily recognized by others. And Neal picked up that slack. He didn't find any problem about talking about Jeff behind his back. When I was in Neal's room studying—or just shooting the breeze, listening to records, he would say, 'Don't you like the way his eyebrows meet above his nose,' or 'I've noticed you can see his rib cage when he wears that shirt.' It was odd to me to talk about another guy like that—as an object of attraction. I had never done that before."

"It's hard to believe we were ever so young," Scott said.

"Or that we were so unsophisticated," I added. "Teenagers today are so much more knowledgeable about every kind of sexuality and fetish than I was when I was eighteen. It's mind boggling."

"So what you're saying is you noticed his psychotic behavior even back then," Aiden said.

"I wouldn't label it psychotic," I answered. "Not then. Curious, like many of us were when we were that young, but also opinionated, like he had already made his mind up on what was attractive to him and what was not. But he could also come off as obsessive. I remember even Jeff picked up on that. He said to me one day about Neal, 'That guy gives me the creeps sometimes. Like he's always studying me.' This was when we lived off campus together our junior and senior year. Jeff and I shared an apartment and we were sort of involved with each other. We had separate bedrooms for appearances sake, though we often slept with each other when Jeff was not entertaining another guy or out tricking with someone else. I suppose our relationship was an open one, though it strikes me more now as dysfunctional, but that's getting a bit off the point of Neal. Neal would sometimes come over to the apartment after classes with one of us and stay for dinner. Better yet, now that I recall it all, he would cook for us. Elaborate dinners he made from special ingredients he brought and cookbooks he lugged over to our apartment. He would offer to cook for us so he could spend time with Jeff."

"You sure he wasn't so drawn to you, too, and not just Jeff?" Scott asked.

"It's true I was a thin and pretty young man," I smiled and answered Scott. "Your boyfriend here just saw one of the pictures of that strange, slender creature I used to be at that age. But I never had those kinds of suitors, not even at that waist size. *Obsessive suitors.* I've always been the kind of guy who other guys said was nice, which usually meant—especially when I was in New York—that I was rather boring. Just as non-descript as Neal was, I suppose, although in an altogether different way."

"You put yourself down too much," Scott said.

"No, not really," I answered. "I don't think I inspire that kind of passion in lovers. Not like you and Trey Weissberg. Remember him?"

"Of course," Scott nodded. "He still keeps in touch with me now and then. Trey was my first stalker."

"First?" Aiden laughed. "There have been others?"

"None quite like him," Scott answered. "He was a real sweetie, even if a bit unbalanced. I met him backstage when I went to see an actor I had once dated. Trey was an intern for a general manager of several Broadway shows and he was star-struck kid who hung out in the dressing rooms, looking for gossip, running errands for the stage manager or the cast. He was this nervous young guy with big glasses and a huge Adam's apple. He had just started college and was something of a goofy nerd—he was interning between his semester breaks. And I was a much older man—almost thirty!"

Scott paused and laughed at his memory. "Twenty-eight to his nineteen. He knew my name from the paper and he was so impressed that a critic was talking to him backstage. He asked if we could have lunch. Then he wanted to see my office and my apartment and, of course, I ended up having sex with him. It was actually delightful because he was a lot of fun in bed because he just had so much energy and just talked and talked and talked, even when he was sucking cock. But he wanted to keep seeing me and I just didn't want to be in a relationship with him—he was so loud and nerdy it was embarrassing being in public with him at times. And I felt a bit compromised by it—the older man, someone in the biz. He used to write me love letters and send them to the paper. All of our mail was opened by the mail clerks to make sure we weren't getting any special gifts or kickbacks. I got a lot of kidding over those letters because they were read by so many people before I ever got it in my hands. But they were sweet notes. I was also trying to seriously date two or three other guys at the time. Not really looking to settle down at that moment, but to find a boyfriend. And I just wasn't attracted enough to Trey to keep wanting to see him. It's a crime, really, that gay men rely so heavily on looks, body type, fetishes, fixations—really go for sex based on attraction more than they do for a guy who might be a really good partner. I'm as guilty as the next gay man, of course. And then there's that New York food-chain mentality—that he wasn't high enough up the ladder for me to pursue *him*."

He laughed again and I noticed that Aiden's expression was sour and perturbed, even though he did his best to hide it by sipping at the coffee in his mug. I suppose he didn't like Scott being the center of attention, or of the fact that he might be considered lower in the L.A. food-chain mentality than Scott, and Scott, recognizing Aiden's unease, shifted the focus by turning toward Harley and asking, "Harley, have you ever had any stalkers?"

Harley arched his back and bashfully looked away from the rest of us, his head titled skyward as if he were studying the underneath of the porch awning for hornets' nests. "I've never been a big city guy," he answered. "So I've never put myself around that kind of scenario. I've had good buddies who seemed to be more than good buddies sometimes."

"There was a guy I chased in Manhattan when I was in my twenties and still thin," I said, helping to shift the attention away from Harley, who always admitted with a bashful shrug that he was not a great conversationalist. "I was crazy about him. Bill Sellingo. That was his name. The first time I saw him at a bar in the Village, I thought he was *so* attractive. The perfect kind of guy I wanted to have a relationship with. He looked a bit like Ricky Nelson, but older and more preppy. Well dressed. Slightly balding. Pretty, but masculine. Beautiful eyes and lips. Dark black lashes. I met him about two years later, 1982, I think, when I took a share in a house in Southampton—a large Tudor near the North Sea. Scott was there. You came to the house one weekend."

"It was a musty old place," Scott said. "There was a dampness to it. Moldy. But it was huge. Everyone had a private room, as I recall."

I nodded and added, "It was a wild place. We always had too many guests out. One Saturday night I'd gone with the other guys in the house to The Swamp—a gay restaurant and bar out near East Hampton—and then walked down the highway to go dancing at The Attic, which was the popular club at the time. He was there that night at the club. Bill Sellingo. Same handsome guy I had fantasized about in the city. I didn't think I stood a chance of meeting him, but he came over and asked me to dance and I ended up bringing him back to the house. I was determined not to let it be just a one-night stand. I got his phone number in the city. Called him up for dinner. We dated five or six times. I remember he had a beer can dick. Oh man, it was thick and painful, but I was a determined young thing and I wanted to make him happy, so I used to practice opening myself up with a dildo before I would go out on a date with him. When it looked like he was breaking away, I went crazy because I had invested all this energy on him. I would walk by his building in the city—he lived in the West Village on Grove Street, on the fourth floor of a walk-up. His bedroom window was on the side of the building but you could see it from the sidewalk. I used to go there and see if the light was on in his bedroom. I was always upset by whatever I saw—why wasn't he calling me if he was home, and worrying where he was if he wasn't."

"Did you ever write about this?" Aiden asked.

"No," I answered. "It was a dark spot about myself that I didn't want to admit existed. And my behavior became worse. I think for almost a year after he dumped me I harbored a resentment because he had not even given me the courtesy of a phone call. He just disappeared. Stopped calling. Didn't return my phone calls. Then I began to call his apartment in the middle of the night, wait for him to pick up the phone, and then hang up. This was long before caller ID, when you could get away with that kind of behavior."

"Did I ever meet this guy?" Scott asked.

"I think I pointed him out to you one night at Uncle Charlie's when I saw him there," I answered. "But I never made a big deal of him because I didn't want to embarrass myself, or show you how vulnerable and wounded I felt. Years later I saw him at an ACT UP meeting at The Center with another guy I was certain was his lover—who looked just like I had when I was that young—thin, innocent, hair for days—brown and floppy, covering the ears, eyes, curling up at back of the neck. The boyfriend reminded me of a younger me."

"There was a guy I used to date in New York who was always crying when we got together," Scott said. He smiled and began shaking his head with light, little laughs. "It's funny now to remember it, even though it wasn't funny at the time. He was convinced that I wanted to break up with him and he would go, 'I'm working on myself,' and 'I'm trying to be who you want,' and 'I'm trying to be a better lover.' Then he upped and broke up with me. Called me up one night when I got home from work and said I wasn't good enough for him, told me I was conceited and passionless."

Scott's laughter broke into a louder giggle which caused all of us to smile and laugh along with him. Zero, feeling left out, jumped to his feet and trotted over to Scott to be petted. "I had a girlfriend who once acted like that," I said.

"A *girlfriend*?" Aiden asked. "Thank God I never went through that phase."

"My behavior was intolerable," I answered. "Very passive-aggressive. I either treated her very well or not well at all. It drove her crazy—suicidal, in fact. Her mother had her committed to a sanitarium. Another dark spot from my past."

"You sure you want to stay with this guy?" Scott asked Harley.

Harley smiled and nodded. "Sure do," he answered with a smile and a gentle nod. "I find imperfection reassuring."

THREE

It took me years to recognize that my greatest talent was not as an actor, but as a listener. Once I had given up my desire to be center stage and in the spotlight, the needy acclaim I desired from lovers also matured into a quiet acceptance that I should not attempt to demand love or something more from my sexual partners other than pleasure. If I could step back and rewrite moments of my life, I would return to the college years I lived with Jeff so that I could hear and share his deeper thoughts and find a closer connection to him. Instead, I was jealous and unforgiving of Jeff's affairs with other men while he was expressing his love for me, and my youthful bitterness and lack of self-confidence often resonated in later relations with my future lovers. But this was also what turned me into a good and honest listener and, once I realized that I was the kind of man that men desired to talk to and confide in more than they wished to take immediately to bed, I soon learned that there was a lot to hear and digest from these men—opinions, secrets, histories, fantasies.

So my opinion of Aiden changed when he asked me, "When did you last see him?" *Him* being Neal. Aiden was clearly not as self-centered and self-absorbed as my first impression of him had led me to believe. We were still on the porch, the sunlight disappearing behind the tree tops, the air becoming more brittle as the wind and cold became stronger. I had believed that Aiden did not wish to talk about Neal any more, had been uncomfortable with my past friendship with him, so I thought it was audacious that he desired to know more about it and made no move to seek warmth—and avoidance of the subject—inside the cabin. In spite of his bitterness over the turn of events, he was also a listener.

"His wedding," I answered.

"You met his wife?" Aiden asked, his expression incredulous.

I nodded and answered, "She didn't make a good impression on me. She was pretty, like a beauty queen—but with a harder edge—like a Miss Runner Up or Miss Almost Made It, because she was trying too hard to be perfect, so she seemed phony and ambitious to me. She reminded me of the kind of Southern belle I was always trying to get away from myself when I was in high school. I don't want to stereotype her, because I'm sure she had a rough time of it in that marriage, but she was graciously cold to me at the wedding. Like she knew everything of my past with Neal and didn't approve of any minute of it, but since this was her wedding day she was not about to be mean and petty and tell me what she really thought of a big-time homo from New York."

Four years after Neal had visited me in Manhattan, he returned to live in Atlanta. He had quit his corporate job in Dallas to open a restaurant in southern Cobb County, near the Fulton county line, within the growing business and shopping district that was being developed between the intersection of the expanding interstate highways and perimeter connections, not far from the suburban area where I had been raised as a boy. In spite of the constant construction, the rerouting of highway lanes, the overwhelming traffic congestion during peak commuting hours, and the fact that the restaurant was outside the parking lots of the largest shopping mall in the area, Neal's restaurant was a big hit—the trendy place to go and to be seen by Atlanta's wanna-be-urban suburban commuters. Neal lived within a mile of his new restaurant, in a duplex near the banks of the Chattahoochee River, in one of the apartment complexes that had a long-standing reputation as a residence for "swinging singles." That was the high-paying young adult crowd Neal was trying to woo to his new place and he managed to lure them in through all sorts of promotions—jumbo-sized happy hour drinks, date night "two for one" dinner specials, "ladies only" coupons. They came to his restaurant with dates or without them, guys on the prowl for local babes, girls on the hunt for boyfriends or husbands; on most nights, nothing too scandalous or risqué occurred, but there was just enough chatter and clatter to make it seem like it was the party-place-to-be.

All this potential romance and sex was what made his restaurant a hit, not the well-advertised huge portions of food and oversized drinks, and through this notoriety Neal became something of a local celebrity himself, photographed for the newspapers and interviewed on local TV shows. Neal loved to find his name in the newspapers as the owner of the place—and that some big shot or another had been spotted dining or drinking at his restaurant—a famous football player, a rock star in town, a super model celebrating her birthday. With the help of a publicist, the restaurant was often used for fashion shoots and television commercials and became a bigger hit, on the lips of most business-tourists and the out-of-town convention crowd with money to burn.

And Neal's self-confidence about his sexuality never faltered. He still went out to the gay clubs in Atlanta after hours—Backstreet, the Armory, J's, and a few other places—sometimes decked out in full leather regalia—vest and chaps and cap and boots. But he enjoyed playing up a sexual ambiguity to whatever member of press might seem interested in his preferences. It became a game with reporters, one in which he always felt he held the upper hand: Was he really straight or not, for instance, particularly when he was named one of Atlanta's "most eligible bachelors" by a local columnist.

Neal also hired the best looking staff possible to work at his restaurant—and he thrived on hearing about their own sexual preferences questioned: Was a too-handsome waiter really gay? Was the beautiful girl with tattoos behind the bar a lesbian? From the newspaper articles I read of him from this time, he had an easy access to both sex and drugs—ludes, pot, whatever was fashionable, but all negotiated in a most clandestine manner and certainly all "under the table." My mother had sent me these articles because she was concerned about my youngest sister Allison getting caught up in all this mess; in a short, hurried phone call one night, I had recommended Allison to Neal and she had taken a part-time job as a waitress at Neal's restaurant her junior year in college. Allison was a beautiful girl, but more religious and unhip than "swinging;" she regarded Neal as an aloof and often absent employer who always "stared a little too hard" at her whenever he was around, trying, as she once told me on the phone, "to see if he can spot you in me." She never bonded with Neal and told our mother he was more of a "health nut than a druggie," because the rumors among the staff was that he was always trying to diet and work out and he now spent more hours at the gym than he did at the restaurant. Allison went in, worked her shift, collected her tips, and left to meet her boyfriend, shrugging off our mother's worries until she had saved up enough money to quit and spend her summer traveling.

When Neal and his business partners expanded their restaurant to a second location near another mall at the northeastern rim of the perimeter, Neal promoted his favorite hostess to day manager of the new place. Her name was Sherry and she was a knockout blond with big hair, implants, and a sorority girl determination. A year later, when the satellite location began going through more growing pains and trying to shift its image from a trendy pick-up joint to a special occasion site in hopes of luring more neighborhood customers and special events, an invitation arrived in the mail for Neal's wedding.

"This was 1989," I said to Aiden. "The year after our friend Kyle died." I glanced over to Scott as I moved through a memory of Kyle, thin and wearing a baggy T-shirt, sitting in the armchair of his Hell's Kitchen apartment waiting for one of us to arrive and clean up the used, crumpled tissues which were scattered at his feet like fallen magnolia petals. "The summer you went to Italy. So I'm not sure if I told you about the wedding or if I told you I went home to see my parents to tell them I was gay."

I returned my attention to Aiden and continued. "Neal had sent me an invitation—it was for a June wedding. An all-day affair at a new restaurant he had opened. I had decided to go to Marietta to visit my parents that same weekend he was getting married. I had been having a difficult time after Kyle's death, fighting off depression, struggling with reasons to remain in New York, since many of my friends were either dying or moving away. Kyle's illness had been a long, drawn-out affair, with everything from KS lesions to dementia." I caught Aiden's eyes and said, "I'm not sure how much of this Scott has told you about that situation, but Scott and I and two other guys had ended up taking care of Kyle when he wouldn't tell his family he was sick and then when he did, they wouldn't take him in or take him to the doctors or help foot the cost for any of his medications."

Aiden nodded and glanced over to Scott, whose own expression remained stubbornly stone-faced, not about to reveal now his own locked-away emotions of that time.

"Scott took lots of trips after Kyle's death," I continued, "but I had two other friends who were ill and struggling and I ended helping them as much as I could bear until both of them died, within a week of each other. I had also been dating a guy, an activist named Dean, who was positive and so full of anger and attitude, and he really did a number on me, trying to make me as mad and angry as he was about the way his life had turned out. He felt I should be out to my parents, which I wasn't. I'm sure they must have suspected something. I was thirty-four years old and they had stopped asking about what girl I was dating. Only my youngest sister Allison knew that I was gay. Dean had worn me down on the subject of coming out, saying that my parents would never learn to accept something that they knew nothing about. So I went home to tell them. I'd always wanted to come out to my parents by bringing home the man of my dreams and saying, 'Look Mom and Dad, here's my guy and we're madly in love.' Instead, I told them what it had been like watching three friends die right in a row, one right after the other."

"How did they handle it?" Harley asked. Harley had only recently begun admitting his homosexuality to the small circle of his family and friends, and his elderly Bible-quoting mother had reacted worse than his father, telling him he was too old to be "fornicating under the eyes of the Lord," what with an ex-wife and two grown children. Harley was dismayed at finding that the "coming out" process never really ended— just when he thought he was done with it, there was always someone else who needed to know or another person he should tell and, now that we were a couple, there was a new level of exasperation to contend with—only two weeks before I had selfishly created a bit of scene in the grocery store in town, motivated, I knew, from all my 'out' years in Manhattan, after Harley had introduced me as "a friend" to one of his co-workers we had bumped into while shopping; I felt I deserved a more affectionate—and honest—introduction—even if the short-term impact meant an uncomfortable acceptance period for him at his company's garage.

"They prayed," I answered him. "They didn't disown me, like many families did at the time. And I wasn't sick myself, just depressed. They wanted to keep my news private and 'only among the family.' I didn't really want to go running down the street with a rainbow flag over my head, either. I think my parents always felt I was going to change my mind about it. About being gay."

"Parents never want to see their children as different from how they are," Scott said. "That's what makes them parents."

"How would you know?" Aiden snapped, the re-emergence of his irritation surprised us all.

"You're right, of course," Scott responded quickly and evenly. "I can only *suppose* how they can feel."

There was a moment of awkwardness, where we all took notice of our moods and breathing and deflected our gaze at Zero, whose tongue was hanging over his teeth, enjoying being stroked by Scott. Then Aiden asked me, in a calmer voice, "But how did your parents handle it when your book was published? All that dirty laundry suddenly surfacing? Their son sleeping with *and* nursing men?"

"Well, it wasn't like I was a media sensation," I laughed. "Not even a sound bite on the late-night local news, and this was a few years after I had come out to them, so they were somewhat adjusted to the notion of having a gay son. In fact, my father wrote me a moving letter about the book after I sent him a copy—sort of a book review; he said it was 'full of understatement and understanding.' He was very proud of it and thought it was a great achievement for me. He had always wanted to be a minister himself, but he had sold out to make a buck as an aircraft engineer and support his family better, so he found great vindication in the fact that he had raised a compassionate son, even if he was gay one. But that's an altogether different story. We were talking about Neal. And his wedding."

"I'm not sure if it was genuine or not," I continued. "If Neal really loved the woman he was marrying. It reeked of a publicity stunt. There was a live rock band playing at the reception, flowers were flown in from all over the country. Sherry had a couture gown that had been made in Paris—with lace hand-stitched by the peasant women of a small town on the Belgium coast—that sort of thing. There were reporters and camera crews filming the ceremony—they had erected huge white canvas tents in the parking lots with fans blowing and a gazebo built in the middle of one where they held the ceremony. People were driving by and trying to crash the reception."

"Everyone sniffs out free food and booze," Scott added and smiled.

"It seemed to me that he was showing people how to do a wedding at his restaurant, not really displaying the underlying affections of why it should be held. I never saw the two of them together except for the five minutes they were in front of the preacher or posing for photos."

"I never enjoy weddings," Aiden said. "They just remind me of something we can't do ourselves—how society excludes us. It's such a perfect moment and all you can see are the imperfections."

"You're just jealous because you're not the center of attention," Scott said politely, but like a man who held a grievance. Now, it was his turn to rile his lover.

"Quite right," Aiden answered and let out a belly laugh. "Always a *bride*, never a brides*maid*. At least you know what you got, sweetie."

"I had tried to get my sister Allison to go with me," I said, attempting to divert the conversation back to Neal's wedding, worried our guests sparring good-nature might turn more wicked. "But she was on vacation that week, with her boyfriend in Aspen. I had asked Jeff, my college roommate, if he wanted to go with me—I would even agree to stay at a hotel with him and help pay the costs, but he didn't want to go anywhere near Neal."

"Can you blame him?" Aiden asked.

"There was never any bad blood between them," I said, not really coming to Neal's defense, but hoping not to reveal Jeff as a petty adult with sour memories. "He just wasn't as close to Neal as I had been. And this was twelve years after we had all graduated and forgotten about each other. I think that disappointed Neal, because he was crazy about Jeff, *always* crazy about Jeff, and we *had* spent four years getting to know each other. But I didn't tell him that the real reason why Jeff didn't come was because he was too sick to travel. He was living out in L.A. and had become a big AIDS activist by then, part of team of guys who ran drugs up from Mexico, and I'd only found out how bad off he was myself when I had called him about the wedding. At the reception, Neal mentioned that he had hoped that Jeff could have made it out too—even though the two of them had not seen or spoken to each other since their final handshake graduation morning twelve years before."

"I'm sure it must have been instinctual," Aiden said. "I disliked him the moment I saw him."

"He looked like a different man at the wedding," I said. "I mean, you wouldn't have recognized him." I turned to Scott and said, "You didn't recognize him, did you, all those years later? This must have been the start of that physical transformation. He'd become a man. Or the image of a man. Not a boy any longer. The baby fat was gone from his face. And his self-confidence really showed. He was quite handsome in his tux—tall, buff. He was wearing his hair in a crew cut and had a diamond stud in his left ear—which was pretty bold in those days to do in the South—I mean, gold chains had barely caught on. Since the restaurant was doing well, everyone thought Sherry had gotten quite a catch. I know I had some shaky moments there, thinking, Why had I overlooked him? Why hadn't things ever worked out with Neal? Why wasn't *I* Neal's boyfriend? I know I was feeling vulnerable, because of upsetting my parents and missing Kyle and Paul and Tony and the fact that I had showed up alone at a wedding, but I sat there and watched Neal get married and kept wondering why I had never allowed us to be lovers."

"At the reception he came over and sat with me while his wife was out on the dance floor, showing off some of her Ginger Rogers moves with a friend. 'Don't think I've given anything up,' he said to me. 'Everyone has their dark little secret.' And he started to tell me about one guest who was a cross dresser and another one who had an elaborate dungeon in the basement of his house in Sandy Springs. And I realized that even though he looked different, his personality had not changed a bit. Not even matured. He knew all the black spots behind everyone at his wedding."

"But I was his oldest friend there," I continued. "There wasn't anyone else we knew from college at the wedding. Just me. None of his friends from Valdosta, when he was a boy. I don't think they were even invited. His family was AWOL. He was never on great terms with his father. His mother had died when he was nine. There was an older sister, but he never spoke of her and I didn't see her there. So I must have seemed a bit like family to him, which is probably one of the reasons why he kept in touch the next year or so after the wedding. He wrote me a long letter on his honeymoon, which I am sure I have in one of my old boxes of stuff because I never threw it away, because it was very descriptive and writerly—quite well-written and emotional, very unlike him. They had gone to London, Paris, and Venice on their honeymoon and Neal wrote me about how beautiful and romantic the trip was but also how conflicting he was finding the experience, because he realized he was not seeing it with someone he really loved. Apparently, Sherry was more intent on shopping and buying gifts then she was on being a good companion for her husband, and Neal had lost some of his own enthusiasm to prowl through the gay clubs late at night by himself—the long hours up to the wedding and then jet lag were doing a number on him. And this was at the height of the AIDS scare—even abroad. People were suspicious of gay American tourists. I remember he wrote with such precision about an evening boat ride they took together along the Seine—something very touristy but meaningful to him. He described the history and architecture of the buildings they floated by—with Notre Dame illuminated with spots and the lights reflecting off the river. And he wrote it was one of his more eye-opening experiences of his life because there was his drop-dead gorgeous new wife right at his side in one of the most beautiful cities of the world, leaning against the railing of the boat saying, 'I heard there is a place near there where you can get great discounts on china.'"

"I'd say he got what he deserved," Aiden said. "But then I'm biased."

"The marriage did collapse first," I answered him.

In one of the letters Neal had written to me after his wedding, there had been a description of the new three-story house he had built in an upscale enclave near the Gwinnett County line called "Jones Mill Estates." "There are more bedrooms than Sherry and I will ever use together—or alone," Neal added at the end of the note. "If you need a place to escape to when you visit your folks, I'd love to have you stay here."

As it happened, it was more than two years after Neal's wedding before I returned to Georgia—I had taken a new position at my firm so my vacation time was tight, and when I was next in Atlanta it was to help my parents pack up their house—they had bought a smaller and more modest home outside Daytona Beach and they were dispensing with all of my childhood artifacts through a series of garage sales—books and baseball bats and original cast albums that I had once cherished and treasured and was shocked to think my parents could part with so easily—and to the lowest bidder. Indignant, I had flown in and rented a van to move some of my boyhood stuff into a storage space near the Interstate and, while I was in town for the hastily-planned weekend trip, I had called Neal to say hello, thinking we might meet for a drink at his restaurant and I could gently break the fact that Jeff had died, in case he had not heard. That was when I learned he was separated and living in Valdosta—too far away for us to rendezvous on the spur of the moment. Sherry was filing for divorce because she was involved with another man—a younger, heterosexual one—and Neal had already given up the house to her. He was also in the process of filing bankruptcy. One of his business partners in the restaurant expansion had embezzled money and the other had lost cash in a real estate scam. He was in a bitter mood when I finally reached him at his father's house. "You can't trust anyone, can you?" he said to me. "I should have hunted them down before they attacked me."

"He took the bankruptcy pretty hard," I told Aiden. "It made him more upset than his wife dumping him for another man. He couldn't believe that he had let his business partners out manipulate him. Steal the money right from under his nose. It just infuriated him to no end. He was very proud of that restaurant and he'd gotten a taste of the good life. Good money. Good times. Happiness. He saw himself as a success so he didn't take the defeat well and I'd always expected to hear some tale of revenge from him. But he disappeared from my life after that phone call. I never heard from him again and he seemed to be avoiding me. Like he was embarrassed. Or just ignoring me. I tried tracking him down once or twice. Left messages on an answering machine. Sent him a Christmas card one year that came back, 'Addressee Unknown.' I always thought that I would hear from him again, once he got his life back into the shape he wanted it in. But then the years went by and I lost the initiative to know what he was doing. The next thing I knew he was dead. I read it in our alumni magazine. It was a small mention, and I got the magazine in the mail several months after the fact because I received it at the office here, in Asheville, after I had moved out of New York and changed my address with the Alumni Office. So there it was on the page of obituaries—just the cold news of it: 'Neal Mullinax, Class of '77, died September 9, 2001.' There was no mention of how he died—under any kind of circumstances or from this or that cause. I called the Alumni Office to see if they could give me some details but they had nothing on file. And no one really wants to talk about that kind of thing—even when they do know about it."

Aiden shifted uncomfortably and I knew it was time for me to change the subject. He deflected his eyes to the wicker weave of the arm of his chair while I brought my tale to its conclusion. "Then there was a day when I thought I might be able to find something about him on the Internet," I said. "How he died. There were several news items about it in the Atlanta papers. But it wasn't until I read one of Scott's e-mails about two or three months ago that I realized that your sister's court case was related to Neal's death and all the pieces fell together. I'm certainly not trying to convince you that Neal was a different person than who he was or who he became, only that I knew him as a friend and not anything else."

"It's unnecessary suffering," Aiden said. "Another tragedy on top of an unnecessary tragedy, in my opinion. I wish my sister would drop her lawsuits, but she can't let go."

"And no one can blame her for that," I answered. "Any of us in the same circumstances would probably act the same way."

Harley dropped his legs from the porch railing to the deck, stood up and stretched his back. Zero popped up from his position at Scott's feet and leapt his front paws up onto Harley's thighs. "Sun's gone down," Harley said. "I can start the fire inside."

"Let me help you in the kitchen," Aiden said. "Give me something to do."

FOUR

"Are we expecting the Royal Family?" Aiden asked.

While Harley started the fire in the hearth of the Great Room, Aiden and Scott had followed me into the kitchen, Zero close behind them, delighted by the change in rooms and hoping it meant food for him. Scott had the good sense of staying out of the way, stooping down to his haunches and petting Inky, but Zero stayed eagerly at my side, convinced that I would feed him something if he just looked up at me with his sad eyes and begged. Aiden, too, had decided to hover close beside me, reading my recipes which were hand-written on the back side of a stack of green-colored index cards which listed, in order of succession, the Kings and Queens of England.

"I've used these since college," I answered him. "Junior Year. History of the British Empire. I can do the Plantagenets, Yorks, Tudors, and Stuarts, but the Hanovers still throw me."

"You might have a great marketing scheme here," Aiden said. "Learn world history while you cook."

The first Thanksgiving dinner I cooked for friends was the year Jeff and I shared an apartment off-campus. I was not a good cook, knew nothing about cooking, really, and had already developed a reputation among my friends as a bad one from the time I had cooked frozen broccoli with a half-cup of salt for a dinner party of six. (The recipe on the back of the box had instructed to boil the broccoli shoots in a half-cup of salted water, which I had taken, literally, to mean a half-cup of salt.)

There were to be five of us that year for Thanksgiving dinner, 1975—myself, Jeff, Neal, and two girls from the University choral group who had not traveled home during the break in classes—Lee-Anne, a statuesque sorority girl, and Tracey, a short, overweight brunette who had a crush on Neal. I had called my mother to tell her I would not be coming to the house for the holiday and would be eating with my friends and in the same breath asked her for her recipes, which I wrote down on the back side of index cards I had been using to outline the royal succession to the throne of England. This was long before the Internet, of course, and I had spent close to an hour with my mother on the telephone, writing down how to wash and baste a turkey, how to prepare the stuffing, how to make a string bean casserole and a cranberry Jell-O salad, when to start making the gravy, when to heat the pie—all the things I had never paid attention to when she had done it for our family. That meal had turned out fine once Neal had decided that our oven did not cook at the temperature it read on the dial, though there had been a bit of a squabble over dessert as I recall, or, rather, a bit of a broken heart when Neal told Tracey that she had put too much sugar in the frosting of a cake she had made for the occasion and she had reacted by breaking into tears.

"No cookbook?" Aiden asked. He looked alarmed. Or mock-alarmed, as if I were the queerest gay man ever to step foot in a kitchen without a professionally-written bible of what to do. I was not about to admit to him that I was a lousy cook—that Harley generally did all of the cooking for us on the outdoor grill when the weather was fine and that my idea of a well-balanced meal was to eat out at a restaurant. Instead, I answered rather proudly, "Every year I add a little something different."

I picked up one of the cards from the stack, flipped it over, and said, "This was '98, I made an apple cobbler that year for a guy I was dating—Russell—who turned out to be a bit of a rotten apple, himself—but the pie was great. And this was '87—the year Kyle ordered an organic turkey. Scott was there for that one. The pan had a hole in it and we had a terrible smoke problem in the apartment."

Scott looked up from the floor and Inky and said, "Kyle was in such bad shape it didn't bother him. The rest of us were coughing and our eyes were tearing."

"And this year?" Aiden asked.

"A pumpkin pie."

"A *real* pumpkin pie?" Aiden asked, again with his mock-alarm expression and tone of voice.

"Of course not," Harley answered as he walked into the kitchen and rinsed his hands at the sink. Zero quickly abandoned me knowing for certain he could expect a treat from Harley. "It's from a can."

Aiden turned to me and asked, with a disappointing tilt of his head, "And the crust?"

"Store bought," Harley answered again for me. "But he bakes it up all just fine." He reached into a box of dog treats and held one up in front of Zero's eyes. The dog leapt up and snatched it from Harley's fingers, did a little circle on the linoleum, his paws clacking-clacking-clacking till he settled into a corner and began gnawing at his bone.

I was eager to get the topic of discussion away from my cooking skills, worried that sooner or later Scott might dredge up a memory of burned waffles from the summer house in the Hamptons, and I asked Aiden if he was ready for a cocktail yet.

"On an empty stomach?" he answered. "I shouldn't!"

"You should," Scott said. "It'll calm you down. And I'll join you."

While the three of them hustled about the kitchen—Harley pulling down glasses and ice cubes and showing them our supply of liquor and mixers, I threw away the cans of cream of mushroom soup that I had used to make the green bean casserole and tried not to feel like too much of a cooking fraud. I'd never admit that I was a sentimental man, because I wear my sentiment like a protective apron, and these note cards represented close to thirty years of my holiday memories that I had religiously refused to let go of—the stain on the recipe for gravy was from the year I'd cooked for my cousin and her boyfriend the first year I landed in Manhattan; the burned edges on the card for the recipe for stuffing was from the year I cooked the organic turkey for Kyle and, while rescuing the burning turkey pan, the card slipped too close to the gas flame.

Kyle had always gathered his friends for a home-cooked meal at his apartment during the holidays and it was my intention to keep up the tradition the year he was too ill to do it himself. I had met Kyle at a holiday party on the Upper West Side, one of those friendly but over-crowded gatherings that take place in apartments on West 77th Street on the Upper West Side on Thanksgiving eve, when the giant cartoon-character balloons are blown up along the block for the next day's parade. Snoopy, Kermit, Popeye, and Mighty Mouse were lumpy rolls of rubber when I followed Scott into a doorman building and took the elevator to the 17th floor. Kyle, who was a friend of the actor who had lucked into subletting the apartment, was standing near the windows looking down at the saggy bloat of Popeye's forearm and calculating the net worth of the view when Scott introduced us to each other.

Kyle had long, limp, reddish-brown hair, a high forehead, and small dark brown eyes brightened by the glint of the bookish, silver wire-rimmed eyeglasses he wore. His face was too strong and serious to allow his impish sexuality to become annoying, but because he was always meticulously groomed— hair evenly cut around his small ears, his jaw closely shaved and with a whiff of aftershave at his collar—it was difficult not to fantasize undressing him.

I had gone home with Kyle that night to his apartment in Hell's Kitchen and had stayed until the next morning, when he awoke cranky and hung-over and hurriedly tried to get rid of me before he began cooking his holiday meal for "eight or nine of his dearest and closest friends," one of whom was Scott and to whom I protested to later that night on the phone when he had returned to his apartment stuffed and tired from Kyle's elaborate holiday feast. "He didn't even have the decency to ask me if I had any plans of my own," I said, though I was not dismayed that I had been overlooked and ignored—at that moment I was simply a one-night trick for Kyle and I had certainly treated some of my other sexual partners worse than Kyle had treated me. And the truth was I did have plans of my own in place, though I was also somewhat miffed that Scott had chosen to dine with Kyle and his fabulous crowd of in-the-know urbanites instead of with me and my cousin from Westchester and her new boyfriend, though I couldn't blame him for his choice. (Ours was an awkward dinner, made even more uncomfortable by my cousin's boyfriend's visible disdain of an openly gay man.)

Kyle and I dated each other a few more times that holiday season, but I found him too passive in bed and too pretentious out of it to want to be boyfriends with him. And, since we had so many good friends in common (not to mention several of the same ex-boyfriends), we soon became closer friends than significant others, brothers, really, instead of lovers, more able to tolerate each other's faults. Scott and Kyle had also cultivated a gently antagonist relationship which I enjoyed being an audience for, since it was often carried out as if they were characters in a play. Scott was traditional, structural, and habitual; he grew up with old Southern money, debutantes in white gloves, and mint juleps on the plantation porch, that sort of thing, and his opinion was often based on etiquette and education, both social and literary. Kyle, however, was faddish and trendy—always on the run to visit whatever gallery or restaurant had been anointed as *au courant* and *en vogue*. They often passionately disagreed on the arts, particularly on new wave films or avant-garde plays that Scott had negatively reviewed—"I'm sorry, Kyle, but where was the plot?" Scott would argue, or "It was a lovely melody, yes, but the dialogue was out of a soap opera." Kyle, in turn, would huffily respond, "Don't be so small, Scott, learn to think outside of the box!" or "You're condemning it simply because it's different, not because you don't want to admit it was good."

And, as fate would have it, Kyle and Scott became my surrogate family in the city, and for several years later, when I *had* been invited to attend Kyle's holiday soirees (where I had also helped him cook), I would often kid him that he had thrown me out in favor of his more wealthy and snobbish friends, all of whom seemed to change or just simply disappear from year to year. Kyle had many famous friends, in fact, including several Broadway actors (one of whom was a Tony winner), a Soho gallery owner, and several writers at work on various new projects—all of whom I would never see or hear about during the year until these annual holiday gatherings. Kyle also liked to be pretentious with his menu, using olive oil imported from Greece, for instance, because it had a more fruity taste, or buying imported black Himalayan truffles because they were less pungent than the European brands, but by then I had grown to consider his pretentiousness more ironic than serious, a faux-pretentious, as it were, particularly when he would describe the hors d'ouevres of shrimp wrapped in seaweed as Asian fusion or explain that the chunky tomato pasta sauce was prepared the way it was in a particular hill town in Campania.

But Kyle was a much better host than I ever learned how to be; he didn't fret or hover as I did; he laughed and nodded, placed his hand on shoulders, interrupted conversations to refresh drinks. And he was much more hip and cutting edge than I ever cared to be, always quick to ask his guests, "What's been going on with you?" or "Kindly give me all of the details, please, you know how interested I am in all of this." I attributed his sense of ease with having been a life-long New Yorker and a product of a broken home, living in a succession of Manhattan apartments with either his mother or father and learning to impress their parade of suitors with his charm and quick wit.

All of his famous and long-standing family friends evaporated when he became ill, of course, or, rather, as he progressively deteriorated from AIDS, a secret which he kept hidden from his parents as long as he could (but which did not escape their prying eyes). Scott and I were left monitoring his doctors and medicines and disclosing the truth to anyone we could find to tell it to, both close and casual, professional or medical, especially when Kyle took a leave of absence from his job as a publicist after an extensive hospitalization for a variety of items which no doctor could seem to pinpoint the exact cause of, except from an ever-weakening immune system.

After his death, I had tried to keep up Kyle's Thanksgiving tradition going for as long as I could, but his glittery crowd was not interested in re-assembling for such a sure-to-be morbid gathering of my bad cooking, and as more of my own friends were lost or moved away or became involved with other partners, my Thanksgiving routine became more intimate again, usually entertaining my boyfriend-of-the-moment by candlelight and a simple meal, if he were in town and willing to be subjected to my cooking. Now, after so many years of Thanksgiving without him, my memories of Kyle seemed reduced to smells and stains on recipe cards.

"You know how to cook a pecan pie?" Scott asked. It was his turn to hover about me, drink in hand, looking at the note cards.

"I tried it one year," I said. "Not much success."

"What kind of Southern boy are you?" Aiden asked. They had changed places; now, Aiden was now on his knees petting Inky and looking up at me from the floor. "Don't you know you're supposed to doctor it up? More rum the better."

"Or bourbon," Scott added, close behind. "That's how my mom always did it."

"Touché," Aiden said, and raised his glass in the air, his face breaking into a bright smile.

"Who's Mitch?" Scott asked, still thumbing through my note cards. "Did I ever know a Mitch?"

"What do you mean?" I answered him, feeling the blood drain from my face. I did my best to hide my astonishment as I took the notecard from him and looked at where I had scribbled in pencil, years before, "Call Mitch."

"He was a guy I met when I first moved to the city," I answered apprehensively, shifting my eyes away from the card to hide my surprise of finding his name there. "I was supposed to get together with him Thanksgiving night. I guess I never erased it."

That, of course, was the short version of my friendship with Mitch, but there was a longer and more problematic shape to it that I had never admitted to anyone. Mitch had big blue eyes, wavy black hair combed back to emphasize his widow's peak, and a compact, lean body as suggestively obscene as a porn star, full of pulpy veins snaking across the muscles of his arms and thighs. He had nothing of Scott or Kyle's refinement, the son of a steel worker and the last child in a family of six in northern Pennsylvania. I had met him when we were both leaving the Club Baths on First Avenue one Sunday morning in 1978 and he had asked me if I had met anyone interesting (which I hadn't) and I asked him if he wanted to join me for breakfast at a diner (which he did). There was an intense moodiness to him, though his speech was often short, staccato phrases and rarely a complete sentence. I was fascinated with his hyper-masculinity, the black, pebbly stubble of beard to the glossy dusting of black hair at the back of his knuckles. I always believed that since we had met coming out of a sex club that Mitch thought me more of a hedonist and sexual athlete than I truly was, an illusion that I dishonestly tried to carry off as best I could. He had a complete lack of sexual inhibition and, along the course of our friendship, I followed him through a maze of discos and backrooms in the city, places I would have never had the courage to go on my own because I wanted to be with him, wanted him to say, "Let's just forget about all this nonsense and go back to my apartment and do it together." Which, of course, never happened.

In many ways, this warped mentor-protégé experimentation was an extension of the relationship I had enjoyed with Jeff only a few years before, and Mitch hungrily summoned up my passion to please a handsome partner. I would have settled for giving him a blow job just once, but he was completely indifferent to my desire for him, or, rather, he had no inclination to spoil the "special friendship" he felt that he could share with me, which in his version of the story meant that I was an asexual witness to his self-gratification. Often, after coming home from the baths or a sex club where I had gone with him and watched him disappear the moment he slammed the locker door shut, I used to dream about him fucking me and crushing me beneath the weight of his body. I soon grew tired of my voyeuristic role in his life, however, and months would pass before he would call and I would again agree to follow him out into the night.

This went on for years, of course, in its perversely passive-aggressive way, until the Thanksgiving in 1987 that Kyle was too ill to cook, when one of Mitch's sisters left me a message inviting me to a party at his apartment that night. I understood immediately the subtext beneath the purpose of her call; Mitch must have been too bad off himself to call me. Or too embarrassed to withstand my questioning. The last time I had seen him was almost a year and half before when we had gone to a bar on Columbus Avenue together and I had noticed a rough, reddish patch of skin just to the left side of the cleft in his chin. It wasn't until I listened to his sister's message on my answering machine that I grasped what he had told me was an infected gash while shaving was instead a KS lesion and his health must have deteriorated in the time I had not seen him, in much the same way Kyle's had. I could not make it to his apartment that night, and had written down "Call Mitch" to find a moment to call him from Kyle's apartment, but with the smoking pan and the burning notecards and Kyle's rush of diarrhea before dessert, I had completely overlooked it. When I remembered a few days later, there was no answer when I called Mitch's apartment and, when I happened to walk by his building on 19th Street a few months after that, I noticed that his name was no longer on the door buzzer and figured he must have moved back to Pennsylvania, or worst, become another casualty of the epidemic. I remember the terror I felt as I walked away from his doorway; with the diagnosis of each friend, I felt suspect and guilty of my own health. Everything seemed less rational in those years. And part of my horror was that I had no one who knew of my friendship with Mitch—he was simply not part of my close circle of friends, nor would he have ever felt comfortable there. He belonged to those idyllic days when I had first arrived in Manhattan and the pursuit of sex could be an adventure, even though my larger quest had always been for something and someone more consistent and substantial.

Years later, both Scott and Harley must have realized the guilt of my secret while I avoided their stares in the kitchen of the cabin; I've never been a man who could easily hide his emotions and I had frozen in thought looking at my years-old handwriting for some kind of clue to the man who had once wrote those words. Scott would have pressed me for more details if Harley's instinctive protectiveness had not kicked in first. "When did the two of you last see each other?" Harley asked. He was referring to Scott, of course, not Mitch, bringing our friendship to the forefront of our conversation—and my mind.

Scott lifted his eyes away from the notecard and realized that Harley had directed the question toward him in an effort to change the subject. "Vegas, right?" Harley said, glancing at me.

"Just before the Millennium," I answered.

"Five years ago?" Scott said, imitating Aiden's way of displaying a mock-surprise—eyes bugged out, eyebrows lifted, lips rounded into a small, open "O."

"Has it been that long?" I answered.

Four years before, 1999, instead of cooking and entertaining each other for the holiday, Scott and I had met up in Las Vegas for a week, at a time when we were both single and needing to get away from the complexity of our lives. We had wandered from casino to casino like stoned-out zombies, neither of us interested in the flashing-screeching-dinging slot machines, silently riding the monorails from Mandalay Bay to MGM Grand as if we were floating in a helium-filled balloon, regarding the bright, garishly decorated casino lobbies of the hotels as if they were filled with priceless items of art. We had gone to one of those early bird all-you-can-eat buffets, then saw a show—a Cirque du Soleil spectacular full of flying contortionists and inexplicable electronic sounds, then watched the dancing water fountains in front of the Bellagio Hotel and called it a night, retiring to our separate rooms and falling asleep as soon as our heads hit the pillow. It was a pleasant trip, neither of us even concerned where the nearest gay bar was located—both of us having been burned out by bad lovers that year.

While Scott continued to describe Vegas to Harley, I rinsed and shredded the lettuce at the sink and drained the excess water with a salad spinner, my own memory flowing from Vegas to Mitch to Kyle's smoky apartment, while the others in the kitchen moved between the notecards, the dogs, and the refrigerator.

"Are you okay? Harley asked a few moments later when I had frozen into place. I had filled a ten-quart ceramic tureen in the shape of a pumpkin with the lettuce, carrots, mushrooms, and tomatoes and was not focused on what I should do next. "Do you need any help?"

I was trapped in another moment of sentiment; the pumpkin tureen had once been Kyle's; it was something I had taken from his apartment after he had died because it was such a familiar part of his holiday gatherings when Scott and I were sorting through his possessions to toss away, give to friends, or donate to charities.

I looked at Harley, tried to find a way to describe this, then realized it was another thing I wanted to keep secret. "I'm fine," I answered, shaking the remaining water on my hands into the sink. "I think we're almost ready to eat."

FIVE

The Great Room was stuffy—what with the fire going in the hearth and the heat from the cooking spilling out from the kitchen. While Scott lit the candles on the table with his cigarette lighter, I went around and opened the windows and cracked the door wide enough to let in some cool, fresh air, noticing that outside the cabin the mountain slopes and trees were now nothing but dark lines etched against the night. Harley had gotten Zero to settle down in his spot between the desk and the bookcases, and he thumped his tail against the floor as I passed by him.

"Let me know if you're in a draft," I said to Aiden. I had placed him at the end of the table closest to the front door, with Scott at the opposite end.

He nodded and said, "Are we eating all of this *now*?"

I responded with a nervous laugh. Harley and I seldom entertained others at the cabin and I had clearly overcooked for the four of us—a fat brown turkey lay at one edge of the table and there was a large wooden serving bowls full of corn and onions, apple sourdough stuffing, and biscuits which I had unrolled from a pre-mixed container and heated in the oven. The cranberry Jell-O mold I had arranged on a bright blue serving plate in the shape of a fish which had once belonged to my grandmother, and I had taken the sweet potato soufflé and the green bean casserole right out of the oven and placed the hot Pyrex dishes on blue tiles I had bought during a trip to Amsterdam. I had tried to make the table as colorful and festive as I could possibly do in an understated sort of way—there were matching blue and green cloth napkins and place mats, orange candles to compliment the pumpkin tureen full of fresh salad, ceramic salt and pepper shakers in the shape of turkeys and pilgrims, and three polished silver gravy boats full of gravy or salad dressing. In the center of the table stood a cut glass bowl with an assortment of pine cones I had collected from the mountain slopes during the previous days, arranged in a tower as my mother had once done, years before, when I was a boy.

"Should we say a blessing?" Harley asked, looking at our guests for a reaction.

"A blessing?" Aiden asked, his eyes wide with surprise at the suggestion.

"That would be nice," Scott said, nodded and bowed his head toward the table.

I hadn't expected there to be a need for such a thing, and Scott's response took me by surprise. I had long ago left behind any outward pretenses of religion; prayers and blessings were only internal hopes and silent desires. Faith was health, a day without questioning if a doctor was needed, merely believing that the body could survive the confusions of its mind. There was an awkward pause as each of us glanced down at the shiny, empty plate in front of us and waited for someone to begin a benediction. As I struggled to think of some appropriate words, Harley took over while the rest of us faltered, saying, "Thank you, Lord, for all that we are about to receive. Let us be truly thankful. Amen."

There followed a murmur and a clearing of voices and Harley lifted his head and began carving the turkey, asking Aiden whether he preferred dark meat or white. He seemed quite at ease now that he had a task at hand, and he asked Aiden what portion he would like, wing or breast. Aiden replied and rose from his seat and held his plate up near where Harley sliced at the breast of the turkey. Instead of returning to his seat with his portion of meat, he became Harley's helper, passing his plate of food to Scott and Scott exchanging it for his empty one. Harley used the pause in his task to ask Aiden if they had eaten a big holiday dinner at his sister's house.

"She went through the motions," Aiden answered, taking another plate full of turkey carvings and handing it to me. I was relieved to see that Aiden had not tensed up again at the mention of his sister and that he had not responded to Harley as bitterly—or as coldly—as he had before. In fact, he seemed eager and ready to talk about it, as if my own ramblings and the cocktail he had fixed had loosened his inhibitions and prejudices. "Everyone's still walking around on egg shells, of course," he added. "I can't say that I don't blame them for acting that way. My nieces are pretty good about getting around it. Emma, the oldest girl, is married now, so she's not at home. Ashley, the baby, is already out of high school and planning to get married next year. They both found good ole boys, just like their dad."

When the last plate was full of meat, Harley placed the carving knife on the side of the dish and lifted the bowl full of dressing and passed it to Scott. Aiden took his seat and continued talking, using a napkin to pat away the perspiration around the base of his neck.

"I tried to be a good uncle," Aiden said. "To all of my sister's children. I'm also their godfather. My sister was determined for us to stay close, since we lost our parents when we were young, so she always tried to keep me a part of her family when she got married because she was all I had. She was seventeen when she married Dave, right after high school graduation. I wasn't crazy about the guy she wed—I was thirteen at the time and upset at losing my sister, even though they didn't move far away—just to Huntington. Perry was her second son and since I was just fifteen I felt more like I was an older brother to those boys than their uncle. Bert, her oldest boy, was almost two at the time, so I helped her out with him since Dave was pretty much a useless husband and dad—he couldn't even replace the toilet paper in the bathroom—it had to wait for her to do it—God knows, what he used until then—I shudder to think.

He let out a bit of a giggle, took another sip of his drink, and accepted the casserole dish from Scott. While he spooned out the green beans and mushrooms, he continued his tale, "Bertie and Perry were natural births, but Michelle didn't want me in the delivery room with her. Emily and Ashley were both born by Cesarean—that is such a brutal way for a woman to give birth—and that she let me watch! I stood there and was shocked to see that something so wonderful finds life out of such violence, literally tearing a woman's stomach open to give birth. I don't know how they do it, I have such admiration for them."

"You weren't full of such sympathy for her when we were there this week," Scott said.

"She was distraught," Aiden snapped in response. "And it was driving me crazy to see her still like that after all this time."

When the pumpkin tureen had made its way around the table and back to me, I slid my chair back and walked it into the kitchen to place it out of the way and give us more room at the dining table. An image of Aiden's sister followed me into the kitchen: a woman with swollen eyes, her hair greasy and black, her nose sharpened and pink at the tip from the friction of tissues as if she were fighting a cold. Back in the Great Room, Aiden was still talking when I took my seat again.

"After Perry was born, I used to baby-sit the kids when Michelle and Dave went on vacations," he said. "I was still living at my aunt's house and Michelle would drop them off when she and Dave wanted some quiet time or to go out to a movie. I've always thought that Michelle kept Dave from moving the family elsewhere until I left for college—two months after I started Berkeley, they were living in Atlanta. I always went to their house for the holidays, or summer vacation. My aunt and uncle started traveling more, once I was out of their house— they even came out to see me in Berkeley one year.

"When Bertie and Perry were older, the two boys came out to Los Angeles a couple of times and I took them to Disneyland and a bunch of other places—I felt just like Auntie Mame, fabulous and broke, but always ready for a new adventure! After graduation, I had moved into a house off Santa Monica Boulevard in the Fairfax area with two other guys I knew from Berkeley. The boys slept in my room and I stayed on a sofa bed we had in the living room. Perry was eight and Bertie must have been ten. Michelle knew all about my being gay by then and she wasn't too keen on her sons coming out to visit their gay uncle, or Dave was totally against it, as I recall. This was one of the worst years for gay men image-wise—1986—what with so many guys sick and it always in the news. AIDS. AIDS. AIDS. The week before the boys came out Michelle kept asking me if I was okay, if I was sick at all. AIDS was only something I was dimly aware of, even in my circle of party boys, it wasn't mentioned—and I didn't know anyone who was openly sick then, though I did have a friend of a friend at the time who had just sero-converted. I know if the roles had been reversed, I would have been more nervous than Michelle was about having the boys out to my place because the news was so grim and everyone was still so hysterical about how you could get it. But it was a good trip. My roommates were good about limiting their tricking, or at least doing it elsewhere, while the boys were there. We went to Knots Berry Farm with two women I worked with at a temp job I had—and they just oohed and aahed over both the boys and kept buying them candy and sodas and all sorts of things. Bertie was always a boy—a little version of his dad, but I just knew even at that young age that Perry had the gay gene—there was a choral group performing in one area of the park, one of those Young American troops—silly looking do-gooder teenagers all dressed in the same kind of styleless outfit."

Aiden turned his head swiftly to me and said, "Oh, I hope you weren't one of those, were you?"

"I was," I answered, bobbing my head up and down and smiling, "but I grew out of it."

"Thank God," Aiden said. "Well, Perry climbed up on the stage and started dancing in front of them, stealing the spotlight from about a hundred perfect teenagers. It was a truly fabulous moment for his gay auntie—he was such a little star then. Michelle thought that he might be gay when he was young, but she seldom talked about it with me, unless Dave was out of earshot. When he was four or five, Perry used to like to wear a towel around his head because he told his mom it was like having long hair. The Christmas he was seven, he threw a hissy fit because he wanted a doll because his younger sister Emma got a doll. Michelle was always good about trying to handle it, smooth it over so it wouldn't appear that Perry was becoming gay. Dave wasn't as easy going. He blew a gasket when Perry dropped out of little league baseball because he said it was boring standing in the outfield waiting to see if a ball was going to drop out of the sky."

Aiden paused for a moment to pass Scott the gravy boat and place a roll at the edge of his plate, but after another sip of his drink, he was talking away. "There was a summer I rented an old house between Big Sur and Carmel for a couple of weeks and had the whole family up, including Dave. 1990, I think it was. Bertie was fifteen or sixteen, trying to learn how to surf. When I moved into an apartment near Brentwood, I started having the kids out one at a time because I had a spare bedroom. Bertie wanted to go to Dodger Stadium, and I would do my best to butch it up and take him to a game. The girls always wanted to go to the beach or the shopping mall or out looking for guys, so that was easy and a lot of fun. Perry wanted to drive by and see the stars' homes or tour the movie studios and I got tickets for whatever television show was taping. He was always my favorite to have out because I could see him going through things that I had gone through myself— not recognizing that he was gay so much, but becoming aware of the details behind the way things appeared—like watching him grasp the fact that *Saved by the Bell* was not filmed in an actual school but on these strange platforms with only partial walls and people crawling all around behind the scenes with cameras and microphones and sitting on trolleys. I always put those kids ahead of whatever guy I was involved with because my boyfriends always seemed so transient and flaky."

"Maybe it was the type of guy you were attracted to," Scott said. "You expect a blond surfer dude to be a man of substance?"

"Yes, all right," Aiden said, rolling his eyes. "I got what I deserved pursuing every aloof and elusive guy on the West Coast. It's true, what they say—that you are always attracted to the same type over and over until life beats you down or you learn better. And some of us *never* learn better. I've always thought because I'm a Latino-Italian mongrel that I'm drawn to blond guys, especially New England WASPs who end up in California at the beach. I've got that gene the same way I've got the gay one. I think if I had met Scott before his hair had turned gray I wouldn't have invested as much energy in snaring him as I did, because of his looks. If I squeeze my eyes together just right, I can just sorta imagine him as a blond."

Scott widened his eyes and responded, "Let us all note my partner's use of the word '*energy*' over '*enthusiasm*.'"

Harley reached around the turkey and sweet potatoes for the gravy boat and said, "The stuffing is terrific, Tom," not so much to offer me a compliment, but perhaps to prevent an escalation of temperament between Scott and Aiden.

"I made it the way my sister does," I answered and was overcome with a sinking feeling that resembled a mixture of regret and nausea. Listening to Aiden talk about his nieces and nephews had made me realize how indifferent of an uncle I had been to my sisters' children, even though they had not shown any interest in knowing more about their distant gay uncle than he had wanted to know of them. I had two nephews and two nieces, a set of each by each of my younger sisters. Seasons and holidays had passed without any of us remembering the other,

71

until one day my oldest niece had invited me to her wedding and I had realized how grown up she had become, and how old and aloof with my relatives I had made my own life.

"I remember when Michelle called me and said they were looking at colleges for Perry," Aiden said, not ready to fight with Scott —or drop the subject of his nephew. "I guess he was in eleventh grade then, and I remember how ancient I felt," he added, echoing part of the sentiment that was swirling around my own mind, though I knew he was aware that he was the youngest of the four of us at the table that night.

"He was already so grown up," Aiden continued. "He had come out as gay by then—to himself, not to his parents or to any of his friends at school, but he did tell me when he was visiting me in LA. He was sixteen, I think, that year. Yes, sixteen. He didn't have a boyfriend as I recall—I don't think he'd even had sex with a guy—it was just an acknowledgment about himself. And he didn't have the angst that I had gone through, about whether it was the right thing to be, or if I was flawed or if the whole thing was helpless. It seemed an easy thing for him to acknowledge. And I hoped that I had helped a little bit."

"The bachelor uncle finally becomes a role model for someone," Scott laughed.

Harley and I both responded with smiles and nodding heads.

"Not as a role model *per se*," Aiden added. "But certainly not an invisible presence in his life. He wasn't ready yet to tell his parents. Or anyone other than me, for that matter. 'I want to do it when I'm in love,' he said to me. 'When they can see how happy I am about it.'" He turned to me to acknowledge the similarity of his nephew's aspiration to my own. "That sort of desire never changes from generation to generation, does it?"

I nodded again, but couldn't help noticing that Harley was reaching for more stuffing and that Aiden had not been eating anything at all, only pushing his food to the rim of his plate with the tines of his fork. Scott's appetite seemed sluggish, too, though I noticed he had finished the glass of wine I had poured him and I reached for the bottle and filled his glass. Harley noticed me pouring the wine and asked Aiden if he wanted another drink.

"Another?" Aiden echoed. "Of course."

I motioned for Harley to remain seated and I took Aiden's glass to the kitchen, rinsed it out in the sink, refilled it with fresh ice cubes and good portion of bourbon, the smell of the liquor rising up out of the glass when I added a small touch of soda. I wanted a drink myself, knew that I could handle it, but didn't want Harley to feel like an outsider in his own home by being the only sober, non-drinker of the night, or worse, making it seem easier for him to reach for a drink himself. When I sat the fresh drink beside Aiden's plate, I nodded to Harley and took my seat.

"He was a good-looking boy," Aiden was still saying about his nephew. "Lean, handsome face. Dark brown hair. I remember looking at him one day and going, 'My God, you've got sideburns!' He wore a leather choker close to his neck that he had bought one year at the Dogwood Festival. Left ear pierced. The butch side. He kept his hair short. Very Abercrombie and Fitch. I think I even told him one day he could model—even though he wasn't really that tall. But then, neither was Tom Cruise when he started out. We use guys for fashion spreads who are at least six feet or over and Perry was about five nine. But striking. The kind of guy that girls would notice. Or gay guys would notice.

"He was a good student, too. SAT scores were high. He looked at several colleges up north. Brown and Vassar and Williams. And I met him one weekend at the San Francisco airport and drove him out to see Berkeley, but I could tell he wasn't interested in it. He didn't want to go someplace too far from home and he whittled his choices down to three schools in the South—two were out of state. He settled on the University in Atlanta because it wasn't a big change for him—he'd been to the campus a number of times for senior class projects or a special lecture. I gave him a laptop when he started college—and this was when e-mail was just beginning. He would e-mail me things from his dorm room, or the library, about what was happening at school, or what stupid thing his roommate had done, and then he began writing about the guys he was meeting and dating. It didn't seem that odd to me when he said he went out mostly with older men, because I assumed that by 'older men' he was talking about college seniors, or guys in their late twenties or early thirties who were out at the bars and clubs. When I flew to Atlanta for his college graduation, he told me he wasn't dating anyone special, but he was looking around for someone to get serious about. I couldn't stay more than a day that trip—we were closing the magazine the next day or so and Perry was moving his stuff out of the dorm and back to his parents' house, so we drove both of our cars over to Piedmont Park and walked to the gay bookstore and had coffee and talked. I even told him that if he wanted to look for work in L.A. that he was welcome to stay with me for a while. I was still living in Brentwood and had been dating Scott only about six months by then—so he was full of questions about how I felt for him."

"And which you've changed your mind on about two-hundred thousand times since," Scott added.

"Yes, I regret every moment of our past," Aiden said, then I noticed a new thought wash across his expression. "Scott was passive-aggressive from the day we met. His first day in the office—he was the new guy, remember, even though he was my new boss, he asked me during our first meeting, 'So what are you doing tonight?' not 'Do you want to do something *together* tonight?' I had no idea he was even interested in me and it took me almost three months to realize that he was trying to ask me out on a date."

"But let's also remember that every time I asked you, you would always answer, 'Oh, I'm going to a concert with this older guy who is such a *schnorrer*,' or 'I'm supposed to go to a screening with this *alter kocker* critic.' Guys who were maybe eight, ten years older than he was I found out when I pressed for more details—*men my age*. Then there was the fact of his cubicle at the office. Everywhere you looked there were photos on his walls of young blond boys just cresting through the first years of puberty—not just head shots, but photos torn out from ads or from *Young Miss* or *Teen Beat* and many of the boys were shirtless. It was like a teenaged-girl's bedroom!"

"It's my job to scout young talent!" Aiden laughed. "That's why people buy our rag—they're not looking at the decorating tips!"

"But what man in his right mind would want to place himself up against such competition?" Scott asked. "All these beautiful young gods always in sight?"

Aiden lifted his glass and took a sip, swallowed and then said, "We worked it out, didn't we, sweetie."

Scott swiveled his head in my direction and added, "We're *still* working it out. You know, it's so easy to find someone to have sex with. But it's such a job finding someone to have a relationship with."

"A *job*?" Aiden responded, lifting one of his eyebrows. "You consider me *a job*?"

"Okay, wrong choice of word," Scott answered. "But you know what I mean. We have to keep working at it to find ways to accommodate a partner. We're all middle-aged men here—or close to being middle-aged men, however you want to define that age group—and by now we've all become creatures of habit—we have the right kind of soap we like to use, a certain brand of toilet tissue we like. We use this particular gas station and not another. We buy this item at the grocery store over something else and we get a bit cranky when we don't get things the way we like them. So, not only when we want to date another guy our own age do we have to factor in all the rules of attraction—and sex—but we have to renegotiate all these habits we've accumulated as cranky old men—particularly if you decide to start living together as a couple."

Scott turned toward Harley and leaned his body slightly in that direction as if hoping to make Harley his ally in this discussion. "Harley, you two must have had issues to work out when you decided to live together. None of us are stupidly, romantically, in love, are we? Love, yes, but not the hearts-and-flowers-and-chocolates kind. I've known Tom a long time and he's full of little quirks. Did you know that he's too vain to wear his glasses all the time?"

I laughed at this, of course, and said, "I can't see with them on all the time. I lose my perspective. I only focus when I read. Or write."

Harley seemed too frightened to respond to any of this, aware that if he allied with Scott he could be short-changing or mocking our own relationship. It was true what Scott said earlier, however; it had never been a challenge to find a sexual partner, depending on what kind of guy you could settle for. Harley and I had never agreed on a monogamous sexual relationship during any stage of our courtship; it was more of a 'don't ask, don't tell' arrangement, though there were now undefined boundaries we never approached since we had become a couple living together, such as bringing a trick back to our home. But the truth of the matter was, in my case, I wasn't out tricking anymore—or out looking for tricks. Harley and I had enough sex together—and passion for each other—to keep me away from such a need. And whether Harley pursued other pleasures himself, I could not answer and did not care about knowing. I'd learned long ago that one man is seldom enough to satisfy a restless soul and I hoped that I had moved on to other things to obsess about in my life.

But Harley and I had had to make adjustments living together—there was a difference in our incomes, what Harley could afford to contribute to the mortgage payments and the grocery bills and what I had to make up in the difference. I factored in all the projects he did around the house, though he would not do so in his own mind, which often left us disagreeable with each other or, rather, me so guilt-ridden that

I would have to get up off my ass and clean the bathroom, just so that it would look like I was helping out and contributing to the upkeep of the place. But were we in love? Or was *I* in love with Harley? Yes, but it was just as Scott had described—it wasn't the hearts-and-flowers-and-chocolates kind. Instead, I saw *Harley* as a gift. Something I should feel thankful for after bashing and crashing my way through all these years of my own tricks and lovers.

"I've learned to appreciate whatever I can get," Harley said to Scott, placing his knife against the rim of his plate and reaching for his water glass. "Hearts. Flowers. Even chocolates."

SIX

"The last time I saw Perry was four years ago at Thanksgiving," Aiden said. He had abandoned stirring his food with his fork and now sat with his elbows on the table and used both hands to cup his cocktail glass.

It was too soon for me to start clearing dishes; Harley was still finding pieces of meat to eat on the drumstick he had taken for himself, and Scott, too, was still attempting to work up an appetite—or showing that he wanted to continue eating—now it was his turn to swirl food back and forth on his plate with the side of his knife. I took the opportunity to fill my own plate with more of the sweet potato soufflé, knowing that as I did so, I would most likely be the one of us who would end up feeling stuffed and uncomfortable later.

"We flew to Atlanta that year," Aiden added. "That was the first time Scott went with me. I wanted him to meet my sister—and Perry—show him off to my family."

"The first and last time he's done that," Scott said. "Now he complains about me to them."

"And I have every reason to," Aiden snapped quickly in response. "Because you are always interrupting me. Anyway, this was Thanksgiving four years ago. 2000. Start of the new millennium. Perry e-mailed me before we left Los Angeles and said that he wanted us to meet the guy he was dating, so he suggested we meet up at a restaurant where Perry was working as a waiter and where he could get a discount. I told him, 'Absolutely not,' and that we would take him and his boyfriend out somewhere else, which is how we ended up at The Irish Lad."

"We had only flown in that afternoon, and checked into a hotel that was near Michelle's house—a real cheap budget place on Delk Road and they had given us a room that reeked of stale cigarette smoke—a real ash can—Scott at least has the good sense not to smoke in the house and neither of us wanted to stay in that miserable, disgusting-smelling room—so we complained and left when they couldn't give us a better room and checked into a Marriott that was nearby."

"The room was fine with me," Scott interrupted. "Aiden just enjoys a grander lifestyle than what can be had on a budget."

"It was a dump!" Aiden replied with a rise in his voice. "And there you go interrupting me again! Anyway, we had rented a car and were running late, and instead of seeing Michelle first, as we had planned, I called her to say we had arrived and then we drove directly down to Little Five Points to meet Perry and his new friend."

"Little Five Points?" Harley asked.

"It's a neighborhood in downtown Atlanta," I answered, glancing over at Aiden to see if he was annoyed by my interjection. When he wasn't, I continued. "Full of boutiques and restaurants. It's always been sort of a funky place to be—especially for college kids. A big date place. Trendy and gay. Or gay-friendly. I've never consider Atlanta a 'gay' place like Provincetown. Or Key West."

"We met them at the restaurant on Wednesday night," Aiden began again. "The evening before Thanksgiving. The Irish Lad is sort of a pub in the front and a restaurant in the rear. Very dark. Wood everything. Paneling on the walls. Painted liquor slogans on mirrors. Neon by the bar. That sort of thing—trying to be friendly and low key at the bar, but with a high-priced dining room. Perry and his date had gotten there before we did and were already seated in the back of the restaurant area.

80

I knew, just instinctively knew, as we were approaching them and I spotted the look on Perry's face that there was some kind of trouble between the two of them. Perry's cheeks were flushed as if he had been crying, or arguing. Or fighting. He was winded. His date seemed to have a smug, know-it-all expression on his face. I disliked Neal the moment I saw him. For one thing, he was too old for Perry. He just looked like he had a mean, dominating spirit."

"It reeked of *Death in Venice*," Scott interjected.

"No. He wasn't that decayed yet," Aiden said. "More *Lolita*-like. Only without James Mason's polish, though I could tell Neal's clothes were expensive. And he was wearing a Rolex on his wrist. The whole thing didn't seem right. And I don't think that we held our reactions in too well."

"And you didn't recognize him from before?" Harley asked.

"No," Scott said. "Like I said, he seemed familiar to me. Or similar to someone I had met before. But I didn't recognize him as someone I had actually met before. He was leaner than he was in New York—eighteen, nineteen years before. All that pudgy fat had fallen off his body. He looked pretty buff. He had a crew cut and a goatee and glasses—so it was just a different look. And much better dressed. Very butch-daddy-looking, but in that expensive, imitation-clone way of the 1970s. And he made no mention that I might have met him before. He displayed no indication that I looked familiar to him."

After his financial downfall, Neal had slowly taken steps to bounce back. While living at his father's house in Valdosta, he went to graduate school and earned an MBA in less than two years. After graduation, he took a job with a brokerage firm in Atlanta and was soon managing a branch office after another two years. By the time he met Perry his income and cash flow were greater than it had been in his restaurant days.

"Same evil queen, though, I bet," Aiden said. "I'm sure of that."

"And he made no indication that we had ever met before," Scott said. "My hair had gone gray since I had met him in New York. So if he recognized or remembered me, he certainly said nothing of it."

"He was too obsessed with himself first—and then Perry second—to be aware of anyone else," Aiden said. "I could tell that in less than five seconds. He didn't ask us anything about ourselves, not even, 'How was the flight?' I mean, come on, everyone asks, 'How was the flight?'"

"And how was the flight?" I asked in a light-hearted way, trying to deflect some of the venom I saw rising to the surface of Aiden's complexion.

"Abysmal," Aiden said dryly, averting my attempt to lighten the mood. "We hit turbulence on the other side of the Rockies."

"Neal was quiet in a fatherly sort of way," Scott said. "He only added a few comments here and there about things he and Perry had done together."

"And in a lewd sort of manner," Aiden added. "Full of innuendoes, like 'Yeah, I think you called right after we got out of the shower,' or 'the phone was ringing before we got out of bed.' Like he wanted us to know they were having hot and heavy sex."

"And having it often," Scott said.

"Perry was having a hard year," Aiden continued. "He had graduated from college with a BA in English, but had not found a decent job and was living at home. He wasn't sure what he wanted to do—where he wanted to live. He had missed applying to graduate schools and I don't think he was really that interested in any more school at that point."

"Who can blame him?" Scott said. "He was probably burned out. I was when I graduated."

"He didn't really know what kind of career he wanted," Aiden said. "He hated all those professional occupations, like banking and insurance or law. He had some interest in technology and design—computer stuff, but he had had little college training in it and no practical experience whatsoever. He had been working as a waiter since graduating and he wasn't happy doing it. Though he told me he was working at a reputable restaurant—not one of those fast food places or suburban chains, and he was making decent money. He was planning to move out of the house soon—he was saving up to buy a car first. He'd met Neal at a gay bar one night in late June and had gone back to Neal's apartment and they'd seen a lot of each other the first six weeks—Neal was always calling Perry at the house, picking him up after work—Perry was using Michelle's car a lot to get back and forth to the restaurant. Neal was probably the first guy who had a serious long-term interest in Perry—not some flirty sort of good-looking young guy who could woo anyone into bed for a night and then disappear from the face of the planet. Perry adored being flattered and pampered—who wouldn't?"

"I can remember exactly what we all ordered," Aiden continued. "I had grilled tuna steak, even though we were in a land-locked city and it wasn't even remotely an Irish dish. Scott had a shepherd's pie. Perry had an omelet and Neal had a salad."

"Why do you remember that?" Scott asked.

"Because it was such an uncomfortable experience," Aiden said. "And excruciating to participate in. Neal possessed an intensity that is hard to describe. He was watching Perry's every move—even I was aware of that. But he was also defensive. I remember asking him how long he had lived in Atlanta—that wasn't a horrible question to ask an aging queen—I mean, I was only trying to get enough information to figure up how old he was, even if he were embellishing the truth a bit with his answers."

"Like Internet ages," I added. "Everyone you meet in a chat room is at least six years older than they admit."

"At least," Scott said. "And always twenty pounds heavier." He looked at Aiden, who did not seem to mind the interruption, but was eager to continue talking.

"Neal said he had lived in Atlanta for years off and on," Aiden said. "But he admitted he was forty-five. Came right out and told us. He said he and Perry had a lot of things in common despite their ages, which made Perry laugh and I knew they were thinking about sex again. How could they not be? That's what *we* were thinking about. What kind of sex life they were having. Then Perry smiled and said, 'Yeah, we both like eating ice cream in bed and watching old movies,' so of course I knew that they weren't having good sex—they were having *great* sex—that's what was keeping them together."

"It was sweet to see him looking so bashful at the table," Scott said. "I didn't get as horrible of an impression about the two of them. It was clear to me that Perry was falling in love with Neal and that Neal was smitten with Perry. And as sex goes—I mean, to realize that someone else could be having that great of a time in bed *could* make another person jealous. But we were lucky that we were in our own sort of sexual Olympics at the time."

"Yes," Aiden said. "We were going at it like bunnies, too, but we weren't flaunting it across the table at them because we were too polite."

"That's why we're such good dinner guests," Scott said, his eyes widening with irony.

Aiden caught his partner's look, stopped his tale, and looked down at his plate as if he had been humbled, placing his drink on the table. "We have been rambling on," he said. "The dinner was superb, Tom."

Harley and Scott had both stopped eating and reached for their plates. "We can have dessert now, or later, if you prefer," I suggested.

"Oh, now would be lovely," Aiden said, reaching for some of the dishes and following me into the kitchen.

Soon we were all in the kitchen, Zero included, with the three men standing around the counter watching me remove a pumpkin pie I had been warming in the oven, Zero actually running his tongue along his teeth in anticipation of another possible treat.

"Smells good," Harley said, taking one the clean plates which he had pulled out from the cabinet and pretending to toss it across the room like a Frisbee. Zero, who had been watching Harley's every move, believed him and leapt up in the air, skidding his nails across the floor before he realized he had been duped. He sat back on his haunches and continued to watch Harley, his jowls quivering with disappointment and anxiety.

"We have low fat ice cream for the top." I answered, slicing the pie with a knife. "Or non-dairy whipped cream. Take your pick"

As I prepared the slices to order, Harley began brewing a pot of decaffeinated coffee. There were some more comments about the meal, some more cleaning of dishes, and some questions from Scott on how easily or not I had adapted to a slower pace outside of Manhattan. I mentioned the frustrations of living in the Bible belt and the way the country was now divided into red states and blue states after the recent Presidential elections; the country split between conservatives and progressives.

"Morals," Scott said and shook his head in disgust. Or regret. "What does 'morals' mean? Who is defining 'moral values?'"

"What's one man's kink is another man's blessing," I said. "It all seems so hypocritical since porn is such a big industry across the boards in *all* the states—red *and* blue. The very people who are crying 'moral values' are the first ones glued to the TV set waiting to see a boob exposed."

"But we're just as hypocritical," Scott said. "Trying to shape our lives around heterosexual Christian role models."

"Now, we're heathen role models?" Aiden laughed.

"That's the point," Scott said. "There shouldn't be any role models. What works for a man and a woman shouldn't be expected to work for a man and a man or two women together."

Zero followed Harley and the plates out of the kitchen and into the Great Room, while Aiden helped me with the coffee pot and mugs. Soon we were all back at the table with our pies and coffee, Zero now beside Harley's chair, his eyes expectantly upturned and pleading for a treat. The conversation had changed from morals and role models to ethics and behavior and Aiden was once again talking about his nephew Perry.

"I tried to warn him," Aiden said, pressing his lips against the rim of his coffee mug and gentling blowing across it to cool it down, his voice again full of emotion. "I could just tell it wasn't going to play out well for the two of them. We saw Perry again that weekend. Alone—without Neal, at Michelle's house. I tried to talk to him about Neal but he was skittish, didn't want a lecture from me, which was what I had in mind. And he hadn't come out yet to his parents, so he didn't want to talk about any of it at his parents' house for fear they would hear something and start suspecting him—and there was enough awkwardness there already because I had brought Scott with me and my brother-in-law Dave was floundering about what to talk with us about. Whatever had been bothering Perry the night before about Neal, wasn't on his mind that day. During dinner I would catch him smiling at himself. We were seated at the opposite ends of the table. I suppose I should have been happy for him, but I wasn't. I just knew he was headed for trouble."

"After that weekend, Perry didn't e-mail me as much as he had been doing. I wasn't sure if he was mad at me or unhappy because I wasn't that approving of his affair with Neal. I suppose I went from being the good, supportive uncle to the bad, interfering one. When I called Michelle around Christmas, she told me that Perry had moved into an apartment in Atlanta, living in the spare room of an older man's condo on Ponce de Leon, and I tried to play as dumb as possible on what I knew about the situation. Michelle had met Neal when he came to the house to help Perry move some stuff. He had a some kind of Jeep. Big black status thing. They loaded up some of Perry's CDs, books, clothes, things like that. Michelle thought he seemed polite and respectful, and since Perry had explained that it was only a living arrangement—and something he had found through one of the campus bulletin boards—it never occurred to her that Perry was gay and that Neal was his boyfriend. Or his sugar daddy."

"God, I hate that word," Scott interrupted.

"I have to agree with you on that one," Aiden said. "I'd rather be called 'queer'—which I am only marginally used to as an empowered generic term for the community, since I was heavily taunted by the word when I was a boy—than be called a 'sugar daddy.'"

"You won't have any problems with that one," Scott said.

Aiden turned to Harley and said, "Harley, this is the cross I must bear, and bear it I must—a lover who comes from old family money *and* makes twice as much as I do and lets me know it at any moment."

Harley smiled and nodded and I caught his eye to see if he was annoyed or concerned that Aiden might be aware of our own financial inequality. He didn't seem to be too concerned; in fact, he responded by offering Aiden a compliment. "Well, it must be good to know that he has someone in his corner like you if things ever do get rough."

"*Hardly*," Aiden laughed. "The minute he loses his money and what looks he has left, I'm outta here."

Aiden's laughter—a descending cascade of tones—made us all smile and laugh with him, even Scott. Zero nervously wrapped himself beneath the legs of the table, but again returned to Harley's side, eyes upturned and waiting for food, but all Harley allowed him was another pat at his neck.

"Well, I suppose if I was that young again and some big, hot sugar daddy offered me a place to live I wouldn't turn it down," Aiden continued. "But I should have told Michelle what I knew. She mentioned that Neal seemed to be a bit old to be looking for a roommate—though Perry told her he was divorced and living in a place that was too big for himself. She was thankful that Neal seemed to be a stable kind of man—and a successful workaholic—and she thought he would be a good influence on Perry, make him want to find a better, more professional, job. Mothers don't want to admit that there is something different about their children. I suppose I understand that. It did unnerve Michelle a bit that Neal knew how long they had lived in their house, what their tax bracket was—all this came out in a brief ten minute conversation while toting boxes back and forth—like he had done a credit check on them before allowing Perry to move in with him."

"I called Perry at his apartment a couple of times in January, but I always got Neal on the line who said he would give Perry a message. We were at least back to trading a few e-mails now and then, and I didn't sense that Perry was unhappy, only that Neal was the jealous type. Perry wrote me that they sometimes went to bars together—a bad move, if you ask me. Going to a gay bar with a boyfriend is a sure sign that you're headed for trouble, and since Neal didn't like to dance, he was always getting upset if Perry was out on a dance floor with a guy he didn't know. Perry was kind of showy on the dance floor, too, so I'm sure lots of guys wanted to dance with him."

"I loved to dance when I was that young," I said. "The clubs in Atlanta had big floors and good sound systems. The music was always good at Backstreet. When I moved to New York, I was always trying to find a place that I liked better than that."

"Paradise Garage was my first choice," Scott said. "Though I felt out of place there."

"The Saint was my favorite," I said. "Even without drugs. But I never got that great feel from hanging out at the same place every weekend that I got when I lived in Atlanta. And I've lived long enough to see the club scene in Manhattan morph and change and then do it another dozen times."

"I didn't even know such places existed when I was that young," Harley said. "I was usually just looking for a bar to get away from whatever girlfriend I had."

"You've never been to a gay disco?" Scott asked.

"A few small town joints," Harley answered him. "Where the dance floor is no bigger than a boxing ring—if it was even that big. Never to a big city place."

"You'll have to visit us in L.A.," Scott said. "Twinkletoes over there can take you out to one of those new mega-clubs that seem to be on every corner of West Hollywood now, while Tom and I hang out in the wrinkle room."

"I'd hardly know what to do," Harley shook his head and grinned, trying to stifle his imagination of the place.

"Dance, ogle, wait till all the youngins toss off their shirts," I said.

Harley nodded again and we looked back at Aiden, who was ready to continue his story. Aiden looked as if he were trying to think of what came next, trying to consider what piece of the puzzle to lay down first.

"Scott and I took a vacation together in February to St. Bart's and when I got back to my apartment there was a message from Perry," he said. "He left a work number at the restaurant and I left messages for him there and he called me back collect one night when he was off his shift."

"That must have set you off," Scott said. "I've never known you to accept a collect call."

"And it was worth every cent spent," Aiden answered, his exasperation causing his head to rattle again. It occurred to me that in that moment that Scott's antagonistic approach to his lover was similar to bantering he had enjoyed with Kyle when he was alive and healthy, and I wondered if that was what had brought Aiden and Scott closer together, this sort of invented faux game: argument for show.

"They had gone to Key West and had an awful time and Perry was thinking about moving out and was asking about coming to L.A.," Aiden continued, and glanced at his lover.

"I told you about this. He said he and Neal were having arguments. Neal was working days at his brokerage office, sitting at a desk making hundreds and thousands of dollars, hand over fist, and Perry was working nights, scraping together enough money to buy his own car. Because Perry was never home when Neal got back from work, Neal was convinced that Perry was fooling around on him—always asking why he wasn't back from the restaurant when he was right off work, who was he out with—and Perry's response was that he didn't have to give Neal an accounting of every minute of his time because he wasn't asking the same of Neal. That made Neal go berserk. Neal kept being more assertive and assertive, wanting to know who Perry had been out with—even if it was his friend Claire for drinks after their shift was over. Claire was an overweight girl with too-curly hair who loved show tunes."

"A fag hag," Scott added.

"I hate that phrase too," Aiden said. "It's so demeaning to the girl, because, yes, they adore being around beautiful young gay boys, too, and want to feel as pretty and as important as they are to themselves—I mean, my God, who doesn't? We should punish them with an awful nickname just for that? But Claire was Perry's best friend, and she knew what was going on with him and Neal because Perry confided in her. Every time Perry was evasive with telling Neal where he had been and who he had been out with, Neal would ask again a bit harder, until one night he pushed Perry up against the wall and said, 'I know where you went.' Neal had him pinned and Perry tried to push his way out. Neal was about twice the size of Perry and it just escalated into Neal hitting Perry, a sort of back-handed slap across the face. That sort of spooked Perry and he wanted out. I told him to pack his stuff up and go to his parents' house or get on the next plane to California. But Perry wanted to wait a bit longer, to see if they could work things out."

"It happened again a few days later. Only this time it was at a bar. Neal had followed Perry and Claire into a bar on Piedmont and Neal walked in and confronted Perry about not coming back to the apartment after he was done with work. Neal started being too assertive, trying to push Perry out of the bar, but a moonlighting police officer intervened and instead threw Neal out of the club. The officer wrote down Perry's driver's license number, but no official report was ever filed with the police. But that was the beginning of the trouble because they both had to go back to the apartment. I can only imagine how difficult that must have been for Perry. I certainly would have run away at that point."

While listening to Aiden elaborate his story, a memory of Neal swayed before me like an unexpected road sign materializing out of a dark night. I could see his eyes—the startlingly bright blue eyes, staring straight out ahead of him, unmoved, and I realized that I could not read what was in them—disappointment, regret, terror, vengeance. It occurred to me at that moment that perhaps I never knew him at all because he had seldom let down his guard with me; his self-confidence seldom shattered in my presence, though I had been privy to many of his inner thoughts, fantasies, opinions, and secrets. Perhaps I never understood anything about him. The psychology of him. What made him act the way he did. But if I didn't know him, didn't understand the great human essence of him, did I never know anyone at all? Or myself?

I knew I had to leave the table before my face showed my confusions and the war in my mind was revealed, but I felt shapeless and stunned. I was grateful when Scott pushed his chair back from the table and said, "I need a cigarette break."

My head turned and I followed his departure with my eyes, then joined Harley in clearing the dishes from the table.

SEVEN

Scott returned to the Great Room brushing off the cold from the sleeves of his shirt. "You have a visitor outside," he yelled to me in the kitchen.

"Why didn't you put on your jacket?" Aiden asked.

"I didn't want to," he answered briskly. "I was only out there a minute."

"That's all it takes to catch a cold," Aiden said, as if he expected Scott to begin complaining about his health at any second. "Don't expect me to play nurse."

"I couldn't possibly imagine you even trying," Scott answered.

I'd heard his return from the kitchen when the front door closed and I walked into the Great Room drying my hands with a dish towel, Zero running around my feet, confused over the best location to be—with me or with Harley. Harley was busy adding a new log to the fire and we both turned to Scott and asked, "Who?"

"There's a beautiful calico cat on the porch," Scott said. "Is he yours, too?"

"That's Rascal," Harley said. "You can let him in. Belongs to a neighbor in the valley."

"One of our Christian neighbors," I added. "They run away from us in town because they think we're living in sin, but their cat adores visiting us, lapping up our free milk, rubbing up against Inky."

Scott opened the door and pushed the screen door open. Rascal bounded inside and scampered quickly out of Zero's path.

"He had something in his mouth," Harley said nervously, replacing the fire poker and walking to where the cat had disappeared beneath the couch.

"Oh God," I sighed. "He's forever bringing us gifts." Aiden and Scott were standing beside each other, as confused by the chaos as Zero. "Mice," I added.

"Hand me your dish towel," Harley said to me.

Soon, Harley's hand and the dish towel had disappeared beneath the darkness of the sofa, Zero now tilting his head down to his paws thinking this was the start of a new game. "Come on, Rascal," Harley growled, or perhaps it was the throaty whine of Zero, and Rascal sped out from beneath the sofa and into the kitchen.

"Got it," Harley said, his fist and the towel clenched around whatever small creature Rascal had brought us.

Aiden looked away and nervously said, "Thank God there's a man in the house!"

Harley took the comment as a compliment and reddened as he passed our guests, carrying "the gift" to the front door and tossing it outside, onto the lawn. I had followed Rascal into the kitchen and was pouring him a saucer of milk, when Harley came inside and washed his hands at the sink. Scott and Aiden were waiting at the kitchen door like two little boys, terrified and excited by watching grown-ups handle real life. "More coffee?" I asked. "Or an after-dinner drink to help warm-up again?"

Aiden's eyes widened at the thought of more liquor and answered for both of them, "Why yes, after-dinner drinks would be nice."

Harley looked up from the sink and answered, "None for me, but you have one if you like."

Months ago, when Harley and I had first started dating, I had confided in an e-mail to Scott about our mutual quest for sobriety. Mine was not an abusive social behavior but just the opposite; alone and depressed, I had developed a tendency to drink till I passed out, something I would never do in the company of others—or a boyfriend, if I had had one. Harley's drinking problem, however, was an altogether different story— he'd been in too many bar fights to count and had had his drivers' license suspended twice, something he could no longer afford to have happen while working for the towing firm.

Scott had responded that he didn't believe he could ever give up drinking, even if a doctor had said it would be best for his health. "My health?" he wrote back to me. "I didn't give up sex when they told us AIDS would kill you. Why would I give up drinking? Or smoking? Or pot?"

Back in the kitchen, I poured a small amount of Grand Marnier in two tumblers and considered pouring a third for myself. Because I wanted a drink and because I wanted to escape into a light buzz, I decided against it, and brought the two tumblers out to Aiden and Scott, who were now sitting together on the sofa, Scott's arm draped across Aiden's shoulder and Aiden titled slightly inward against his lover's chest. Harley sat on the brick ledge of the hearth, his arms bent around Zero's neck; his sleeves were rolled up, revealing the wings of the dragon tattoo that colored his forearm that he had gotten when he was nineteen to celebrate completing boot camp.

"Did your nephew ever come out to your sister?" Harley was asking Aiden when I took a seat in the old leather chair Harley had brought from his apartment in Hendersonville. I knew he was doing this in order to find some kind of affirmation or strength to continue on his own path rather than to hear the facts and details of Aiden's nephew. I had briefed Harley on the unfortunate consequences of Perry prior to our guests' arrival this weekend, but had only hinted to him of my friend Neal's part in the tragedy. I still had not reconciled the Neal that I had known myself as a young man to the adult Neal who had terrorized Aiden's nephew.

"He did," Aiden answered. "But it wasn't the way he wanted it to happen. It was sometime in early April of 2001, while he was living with Neal. One night, he called his mom around three in the morning. His voice was muffled, like he had been crying. Michelle heard a girl's voice in the background, prompting him to go ahead and tell her something. She thought it was going to be good news—something like he had been dating a girl and they were getting married, but instead he told her he was gay.

"As if that wasn't enough of a shock for her to comprehend, then he told her that Neal was his lover and he had been beating Perry up. Neal had threatened to call and tell Michelle about Perry's sexuality, and Perry didn't want his mom to find out that way."

I watched Harley's face absorb these facts and change; his attentive expression became abstract and indifferent; I knew he wanted to hear the details, only not be emotionally affected by them.

"Of course Michelle had often wondered about Perry," Aiden continued. "She knew he had some girlfriends in high school and college, but there was no one he had dated seriously. She called me the next day and she was trying to work her way through the news rationally, step by step. 'But he always had girlfriends,' she said to me. I laughed and said, 'Well, so did I.' Even with her having a gay brother, she couldn't keep from stereotyping gay men. She didn't think of him as effeminate or a sissy, for instance."

"Like you?" Scott asked.

"I'll be the first to admit that I am not the butchest of queens, but I am not a nellie," Aiden said, his lips parting into a smile as if he were going to laugh at himself. "She said, 'It's not like he had dolls and I let him grow his hair like a little girl.' I reminded her of the towel—and the Christmas he wanted a doll. Then, she said to me, 'Maybe you took him to too many shows.'"

"She didn't say that, did she?" I asked, coughing out a laugh because I was concerned whether it was an appropriate response.

"She did!" Aiden said. "As if sitcoms and musical comedy could make you gay!"

"They should know every gay boy carries the show tune gene," Scott said. "It's part of our DNA structure, not learned behavior."

"'Maybe he's just experimenting,' she said," Aiden added. "I asked her, 'What do you mean you think he is experimenting? I mean, hello, you have a brother who is G-A-Y. It's probably in his chromosomes.'"

"She wouldn't accept that. 'Sometimes boys experiment,' she said. I asked her what she knew about boys experimenting. 'I know, that's all,' she said."

Aiden let out one of his characteristic giggles, not as effusive as before, but one that was intended to smooth over his underlying tension. "She had no desire to join PFLAG or put a rainbow sticker on her car—in spite of the fact that her brother was a big time H-O-M-O. But she was worried. Perry told his mother not to tell his father that he was gay, but of course she did and, of course, in the typical male passive-aggressive fashion, his father did nothing about it.

"Perry came home a few days later for a visit, and he was wearing a long-sleeved shirt, even though it was one of those blazing hot, humid days that can happen in Atlanta in April. When she asked him about it, he said, he didn't want anyone to notice a bruise on his arm. She made him show her and apparently it was a doozy. She asked him if he wanted to see a doctor—one of the veins looked like it might have been damaged, but he said it just looked worse than it hurt. He was evasive when she asked him how he got it and he would only tell her 'I fell on something.'

"She tried not to worry, but when he called about two weeks later, saying Neal was beating up on him, she handed the phone to Dave and his father told him they were bringing him home. That's how his father acknowledged he knew his son was gay.

"Michelle and Dave drove into Atlanta and helped Perry pack up his stuff. It was the first time they had been to Neal's apartment and the first thing they noticed was that it was small and there was no second bedroom. Perry and Neal had been lying when they said that Perry was moving into a separate bedroom. And the bedroom door was off the hinges—Perry said that Neal did not want him locking him out of the room. Neal was there and he just laughed it off. He wasn't intimidated at all by Michelle and Dave and showed not an iota of remorse for his own part. In fact, he said that Perry couldn't leave, because he owed him money for rent. They started to argue in front of Michelle and Dave and Perry told Neal that the rent wasn't part of their arrangement. Apparently, Neal had been promising to pay Perry's share of the rent for some time, in exchange for his company—not really a hustler scenario, but Perry was 'earning his keep,' so to speak, and so all of this comes out right in front of my sister and her husband. So then Neal said Perry owed him money for the phone bill. Michelle wrote him a check for it before they left. Perry ended up moving back home feeling ashamed and defeated and dirty. I talked to him on the phone that weekend and said he could still come out to L.A. I had just moved into Scott's apartment and I told him that we could find a place for him to stay for a while, that the money I was saving we could use toward his rent. But he didn't want to do it—said it was no different than what he'd just left—he wanted to be out on his own now, paying for his own place, even though he couldn't afford to do it.

"But Perry wasn't happy living at home, either. When he moved out of Neal's place, he changed jobs, too, took a different waitering job—the evening shift at The Continental, because he could make more money than the day shifts he had been doing to make Neal happy, because they were then on the same work schedule. The restaurant was upscale. 'Pricey and pretentious,' was how he described it."

"I went there once or twice when I lived in Atlanta," I said. "Though I heard it had changed hands and menus several times since then."

Indeed, The Continental had been through several reincarnations since my college days in Atlanta. Originally an upscale steak house on the fringe of Little Five Points, which is how I had known it when I was a student, it had morphed into a hip and trendy Eurotrash watering hole with high-tech polished chrome and steel furnishings and ultra-small votive candles on the tables.

"But it still had its reputation," Aiden added. "Perry's commute to the restaurant was long and irritating, because there was always traffic congestion and it wasn't an easy route from his parents' house. When Neal found out where Perry was working, he would show up after work or after he had gone to the gym—the restaurant wasn't that far from his apartment. He'd always get there and order a couple of drinks before the end of Perry's shift and maybe eat something at the bar. The bartender and the owner never discouraged Neal from being there, even though Perry complained about how uncomfortable he felt with Neal around, because Neal was paying in cash and usually buying someone a drink. And he was a big tipper. Nobody discourages a big tipper. Neal always tried to get Perry to do something when his shift was over, but Perry just said no. Neal would follow him out into the parking lot, drive behind him in his Jeep—usually as far as the Interstate. Even if Perry had thought he had given Neal the slip here or there, there he was again, calling Perry's friend's apartment where he was going or showing up at the bar Perry went to—or even worse, calling his parents' house and trying to track him down.

"Perry's father wasn't happy with the phone ringing at all hours, going dead whenever he answered it, and he began telling Perry that he shouldn't stay out so late, because he was waking everyone up when he came home. Perry began staying with friends in Atlanta—Claire and her roommates let him sleep on her couch, or he just slept in the backseat of his car instead of going home so late at night. I think he might even have gone back to Neal one or two nights, just thinking that this might get him to back off a little. But he didn't. Perry wrote me an e-mail saying it was like being in a movie, where the chase scene goes on and on, where just when the hero thinks he's lost his pursuer because of all the zigzagging, there he is again, turning around the next corner and seeing that he is still there coming at him from another direction. Sometimes I'm not sure how seriously he took all this kind of behavior until it started to get worse.

"Neal started to get abusive in a more public way. First, he broke into Perry's car. Smashed the side window and took Perry's knapsack which had his gym clothes and sneakers in it. Michelle gave Perry money to have the window repaired. The next time Neal smashed the lock on the trunk and took Perry's laptop—the same one I had given him when he started college. So Perry went to Neal's apartment when he knew that Neal was at work, broke the new front door lock Neal had installed when Perry moved out, and took the laptop back. Neal called the police when he got home and reported the burglary and said he knew who took the laptop and gave the officer Perry's license plate and home and work address. He told the police that he and Perry had been roommates until he threw Perry out for not paying rent. Neal admitted to the police that Perry hadn't taken anything else, and had only taken something that belonged to him—saying that Perry had left the laptop behind when he had moved out as payment for not paying the rent, but since Perry had broken the new door lock and entered the premises, the officers encouraged Neal to file charges.

"When they questioned Perry later at the restaurant, Perry told the two policemen that he had moved out about six weeks before and that Neal had been harassing him, trying to get him to move back in ever since, and that Neal had broken into his car and taken the laptop. Perry mentioned that they had been lovers, not roommates, and then explained the fights and the bruises and one of the officers jotted it down in his notebook, but asked why Perry hadn't reported that the laptop had been stolen from his car. Perry said he knew who had taken it and had just gone to get it back, then asked the police if he could file a restraining order against Neal, something official and formal that would make Neal stay away from him. Instead, the officers told Perry that Neal was not going to press charges for burglary.

"When Perry explained the laptop incident to his parents he said that the Atlanta police were uncomfortable with him mentioning that he and Neal were lovers and that Neal was abusing him—that all they cared about was that Perry had broken the lock to Neal's door. Dave waited a day or so and called Neal and said, as nicely and calmly as he could, that he should not bother Perry any more. It wasn't a threat, just a phone call, saying, 'We know what you are doing and we want you to stop it.'"

"That's when it all started to change for the worse. It was no longer stalking or constant calling. It was no longer, 'I want to know where you are, where you're going, who you're going out with,' it was, 'I am going to kill you.' Neal would get Perry on the phone, or show up at the restaurant and say, 'You're time is almost up.' It was really scary for Perry. He should have just packed up and come out to California. But he didn't want to run away and I guess no one can blame him for that. He was trying to stand up to Neal. He thought that if he ran away from something like this now, he would always be running scared and that wasn't who he wanted to be or what he wanted to do for the rest of his life. So he kept going in to work. And out with his friends. One night in August, he got off work and he and his friend Claire went to see a late movie at Lenox Square. Neal had been at the restaurant, so they were fairly certain he was following them, but Perry thought he had lost him when they had turned on to La Vista Road. They parked at Lenox and went to the movie. When they walked out later, the parking lot was fairly empty, so it had been easy for Neal to track them down again. He was parked nearby and he got out of his car and chased Perry as he ran toward his car. He caught Perry by the arm and threw him against the Toyota and started choking him at the neck. Claire screamed at Neal, but it wasn't very effective, so she slapped her hands on his back, hit him in the head with her purse, and pushed herself in between Perry and Neal, managing to get Neal to stop choking Perry. As they broke apart, there was a lot of yelling and shouting and threats to call the police, and Perry and Claire got into the Toyota and drove away, leaving Neal in the parking lot.

"Claire suggested that they drive to the police station and report the incident, but Perry said that they wouldn't do anything, because he had tried it already. But Neal had gotten back in his Jeep and was following them. When Perry drove by a police car that was in a parking lot on Cheshire Bridge, Claire told him to pull over. She went and talked with the officers in the car, explaining that the Jeep was following them and 'creeping us out.' One of the officers got out and spoke to Neal, who had also pulled into the parking lot. Neal told the officer that Perry had stolen his checkbook and had made out a check to himself and cashed it. Neal said he was just trying to get his money back. Neal actually had the proof with him—bank statements and canceled checks—and he showed them to the officer and then told the cop that he had filed a report of the burglary of the laptop but had not noticed the checkbook was missing until recently. The officers took them all down to the station and took their statements. Suddenly, Perry wasn't the victim any more. He was the *suspect*."

"Was he arrested?" I asked.

"No," Aiden said. "Neal didn't press charges that time either, and nothing was filed. Perry was released and instead of driving back home to his parents' house, he went and stayed at Claire's apartment, since it was already so late. The officer later told Perry's parents that he could tell that Neal was obsessed with Perry and that Perry just wanted the relationship to be over. But, in my opinion, they had no idea how to handle an abusive gay relationship. Claire later told me that one of the officers wanted the two of them to shake hands and make up, to say that everything was okay. Neal was a manipulative man and Perry didn't want to argue, so they said that everything was fine and they left. No report was written up."

"But it only got worse. The next evening Neal showed up at the restaurant during Perry's shift and threw a piece of cardboard full of holes at Perry and said, 'This is gonna be you.' On the cardboard was an outline of a face and shoulders and the holes were round punctures, as if they were from bullet holes. Perry was really spooked by that. As far as he knew, Neal didn't own a gun, but he also didn't know if Neal had gone out and bought a gun. Perry went back to the Atlanta police precinct with the bullet target and asked for a restraining order. The officer on duty said that since there had been no physical abuse or damaged personal property, nothing could be done. From then on, Perry never walked out to his car by himself. He always had someone at the restaurant walk with him."

Again, I felt something break inside me, a memory of Neal surface in my mind—this time of his smile—his lips parted above his top teeth—part joy, part pride, but displaying the wickedness of a young man. Was in that memory the germ of a man intent on revenge? Or was it just a boyish mischievousness, something we all had done at some point in our youth? Time and time again I had often discovered Neal in his darkened dorm room, quiet and still at his desk, his forehead glowing from the overhead lamp on a shelf, his eyes pinned to the page of a book, or a notebook, or his fingers tapping away at a calculator. Could this have been him, years later, slowly, deliberately cleaning a gun, loading it with bullets, giving it the same meticulous attention he had given his class assignments?

"The next two weeks went by without any kind of incident," Aiden continued. "No phone calls. Nothing. It was like Neal had retreated. Disappeared. Labor Day weekend Perry drove up to Lake Lanier with some friends because he had time off. He came back, expecting calls from Neal, but there was still nothing. He thought it had worked itself out. Then on Saturday night, Neal showed back up and that was the end of both of them."

EIGHT

In the kitchen, Rascal was mewing to be let out the back door, and I pulled Inky and his rug out far enough to crack the door open. Rascal scampered into the black night and Inky, his head on his paws, looked up quizzically at me, the stump of his tail wagging back and forth from the excitement of moving but not having to work an inch at it, and I gave him a pat before setting a bowl of soft food for him to eat. He sniffed at the food, trying to decide if he had enough energy to eat, and then wobbled upright on his shaky legs and began eating with a few laps with his tongue.

Zero was at my side in a flash, racing in from the Great Room at the realization that there was now food on the floor, panting and lurching for the chunks that Inky was too slow to eat. I held him by the collar till I put down a bowl of food for him too, which he gobbled and snorted up in a couple of gulps.

I ran the water at the sink and waited for the hot water heater in the basement to begin to warm up the flow. We'd inherited a bum dishwasher when we purchased the cabin and instead of replacing it, we had decided to invest in a new washer and dryer first. In all the years I lived in Manhattan, I had never had the luxury of a dishwasher; in fact, I had learned to find it quite relaxing to wash my dishes and pots and pans by hand, standing at the sink lost in the flow of memories and warm water. From the Great Room, I heard snippets of Aiden's voice rising and falling as he continued telling his tale to Harley, while Scott made his way in and out of the kitchen, carrying in the last of the dirty plates and bowls, Zero now tagging along beside him, waiting for any sort of crumb to fall to the floor and pounce on it, and rushing up to Inky's bowl when he was back in the kitchen, licking his chops till I pushed him aside and out of the room.

I already knew this part of the story about Neal and Perry; it had been widely reported in the newspapers after the incident, though it had been months later when I discovered the accounts on the Internet and read the details for myself.

It was a Saturday night in September. Just after Labor Day weekend. Perry had worked the evening shift at The Continental and was tired. The restaurant had been crowded, the tips good. He'd waited on a table of seven—a family from Decatur—and another party of twelve—a group of young women celebrating the engagement of a friend. Perry had enjoyed flirting with the girls; they were rowdy but polite, eager to know more about him than he wished to confide. They'd started a guessing game with him—Did he have a girlfriend? What color was his underwear? He'd been able to maintain his privacy through innuendoes, responding with, "Only one girlfriend?" "What underwear?" He had fooled them so well into believing that he might be straight that two of the women had left him their phone numbers, hoping for dates.

So his guard was down when he walked out to his car in the parking lot. He'd left the restaurant through the kitchen exit with Will, another waiter, one of the friends he had gone with to Lake Lanier only days before. Will was from Florida and had a deep nasal voice, but he was more flamboyant acting than Perry's other gay friends, and he asked if Perry was going out clubbing, doing a bit of a twirl as he posed the question.

Perry had answered that he was headed home because he was scheduled to work the brunch shift the next day and he wanted to get as much sleep as he could, but he had stayed in the parking lot talking to Will for a few more minutes, quipping and camping through a variety of subjects from movies to music to the rising prices at the nearby gas station, but always returning to the topic of men—what television commercial had a cute guy in it or had he noticed the hot guy at the window table or did he think the guy at the gas station was a hunk. They parted giving each other a kiss on the cheek.

In his car, Perry turned on his headlights, backed out of the parking space. He had not seen Neal nor the black Jeep anywhere nearby. He gave a short wave to Will, and took his usual route toward the Interstate—right on Monroe, left on Tenth, over Piedmont, Juniper, and Peachtree, listening to 99X or 95.5 on the radio. At Tenth and Spring, he caught a stop light and glanced in his rear view mirror and turned the music down. I can imagine the fear at the back of his throat when he spotted the headlights of the black Jeep pulling up behind his car. He would have checked the mirror a second time, perhaps swiveled his head and looked behind to be certain that it was Neal's Jeep, calculating the potential danger of both the car and his former lover. The Jeep nudged the bumper of Perry's Toyota. Perry felt the push, felt the next one, too. He turned his head around again, this time to be certain it was Neal.

There was no opportunity to lose him; Perry was at the ramp that fed into the Interstate and the journey to his parents' house. He looked in the rear view mirror again to see if Neal would jump out of the Jeep and approach his car, and when he didn't, Perry took the light and merged onto the Interstate, not believing that Neal would follow him.

But he did. Neal followed Perry's Toyota onto the ramp and the Interstate, something he had never done before. He tailgated Perry's car for miles, slowing when Perry did, speeding up and changing lanes as Perry did, nudging the rear end of the car as often as he could get away with without forcing Perry into an accident, but with enough danger and venom to make Perry scared. I imagine it as a taunt, a dare, a challenge to provoke a response from Perry—a way to keep Neal engaged in his mind.

Perry kept his hands steady and tight on the steering wheel, his breathing calm, perhaps saying a prayer or two that he would make it safely to home. He inventoried the car's possessions—was there something he could use as a weapon? Were the keys sharp enough? Could he use them as brass knuckles? Why hadn't he invested in a can of mace? Why hadn't he gotten a cell phone so he could call for help?

Across the Chattahoochee, in Cobb County, Perry took an exit and stopped at a gas station. Neal jumped out of the Jeep and ran up to Perry's car, rapping his knuckles against the side window.

"I'm not gonna let you get away with it," Neal said.

"Leave me alone," Perry yelled through his window.

"You're ruining our lives," Neal said. "I love you. You can't keep doing this."

"Stay away from me," Perry yelled.

"I'm not gonna let you see anyone else," Neal said. "If you don't work this out, I'm gonna kill you."

I can imagine the tone of Neal's voice, the tension in his body, his vehemence and desperation. The vein on the left side of his neck would have been enlarged, pulsing, reddening his complexion. I had once seen this level of his anger appear in the most unlikely of occasions, when he had discovered through an Economics departmental secretary that a professor had removed him from consideration for a campus honors society. But his bravado would have also been apparent on this night, mixed in with a disbelief at the turn of events and a desire to surrender once again in Perry's embrace, to make all things better, to have him back. But Neal must have also realized that whatever love Perry had felt for him was now fading, if not completely over, and with that recognition, he knew he could do anything he wanted to make Perry's life more miserable.

Perry wasted no more time with Neal. He swerved out of the gas station and was back on the road, but it was ten, fifteen, maybe twenty seconds before he realized that he had turned in the wrong direction, headed away from the route to his parents' house. His first thought must have been that he could lose Neal now since he was off the Interstate, take a turn here and then another there, and then make it back home safely another way. But the Jeep was once more behind him, nudging the bumper of the Toyota at the next stop light, Neal threatening him through his window, "You can't do this to us, Perry. You can't do this."

Perry must have remembered then that he was near the mall and a police station. Instead of waiting for the light to turn green, Perry drove through the red light, speeding down the Parkway until he reached the station.

There must have been more words between them in the parking lot of the police station. Neal might have jumped out of the Jeep, saying, "What are you doing?" Perhaps he lunged for Perry's arm and Perry tugged it out of Neal's grip.

Perhaps Perry shouted, "I don't want anything to do with you. It's over. Stay away from me."

"Just come back and we'll make it work," Neal said. "Give me one more chance."

Neal's plea would have made Perry vulnerable; he would have considered going back for an instant, but there was a history of threats, punches, stalking, and now this—this late night chase, when all he wanted to do was to go home, go to sleep, get out of this situation.

Inside the station, Perry told the officer on duty that he was being stalked, that Neal had followed him on the Interstate, tried to run him off the road. He said he was scared of what might happen next. He didn't feel safe—he wanted Neal stopped, warned, told to stay away from him. He said he thought Neal had a gun.

Neal had followed Perry inside the police precinct and was waiting near the door. When the officer, Joseph Grady, looked to the man Perry had pointed to, he stood, smiled, and said, "Neal Mullinax. Good to see you. What seems to be the trouble tonight?"

Neal stood, approached the desk, and said, "Joe. Nice to see you again."

Joe Grady's daughter had once worked as a waitress at Neal's restaurant—just up the Parkway—and Neal spent a moment asking of news of her—Where was she living? (Just over in Alpharetta.) Was she married? (Three years now.) Any children? (A baby girl, Sarah, sixteen months. A handful.) From the photo of Joe Grady that I had seen on the Web, he appeared to be a large man in his mid-fifties—not very tall but with a sizable stomach that showed he spent more hours at a desk than he did on active patrol. When Neal clapped his hand on Joe's back and congratulated him on becoming a grandfather, Perry's shock and disbelief turned to indignation.

"My boyfriend and I had an argument," Neal told Officer Grady, with a sheepish grin. "We're sorry that it's turned into a public spat."

"He's not my boyfriend," Perry interrupted. "And he's threatened to kill me."

"We were just arguing, Joe," Neal said. His voice was steady, without a hint of anger. The self-confidence was back, his composure unruffled.

"What can I do to get a restraining order?" Perry said, his voice rising into a desperate higher pitch. "Can I prosecute him for harassment?"

"Now fellas, this looks to me like this is a domestic dispute," Officer Grady said. "That department's not open on the weekend and there's nobody to talk to till Monday morning." He looked at Perry and said, "Why don't you just cool down, young man, take some time off from each other."

"You mean there is nothing you will do?" Perry asked.

"I could write up a report," Joe Grady said. "If that's what you want."

"Don't bother," Perry answered. "Just tell him to stay away from me."

Perry left the station and Neal did not follow him any further that night. Perhaps at that moment Neal realized that he could go through with it, that his will could carry him forward, that if there was no more "us" for him and Perry, there would be no more "us" for Perry and another man. He tried to be practical, reasonable, but, of course, it was too late and his anger had made him exhausted. If Perry had only insulted him, mocked him, listed his faults, it would have been so much easier to walk away, admit that it was over, and move on. But he hadn't. In all of this Perry had never said an unkind word to Neal. Or about him. And it made Neal believe that he still cared for him and really—deep down—wanted to return and live together and make their relationship work. And so did Neal. Neal's mind became crowded with plans, schemes, solutions, dilemmas. I think that Neal tortured himself into a state of madness because he was unable to find fault with Perry, felt himself going under again, his mental struggle confused by desire and guilt and jealousy. What Perry had robbed him of was his sense of self-purpose, his inner focus, his balance and his goals and his will to live. His self-confidence was shattered, like a mirror which could not be repaired. Neal saw nowhere to go but in Perry's direction.

"That was it?" Harley said, when I walked back into the Great Room. "That's all the cop said? I could write up a report?"

"That was it," Aiden answered. "Perry just walked out of the station, got back into his car and drove home."

"That must have been a big joke to them," I said. "A gay domestic dispute at the county police station, the protectorate of fundamentalism."

"Isn't that where Newt Gingrich was from?" Scott asked.

"Newt, Lester Maddox, and about a million other homophobes," I said. "I'm surprised that they didn't try to put him in jail right there for admitting that they were sodomites."

"It was a joke," Aiden said. "The incident was treated like a joke."

At home that night, Perry's mother, Michelle, found her son in the kitchen, scared and shaken, his eyes glazed over, the events of the night playing out again in his mind. Michelle expressed annoyance with Perry, a look-what-you've-done-gone-and-done sort of response that was more "I told you so" than sympathetic. She gave the impression that her temper could be easily lost if this continued.

Michelle's recollection of her son's mood and manner that evening were also widely reported in later news accounts. He was near tears and flushed with fear on what he thought might happen next. Perry told her he was tired of running from Neal, tired of driving every day back and forth to Atlanta, tired of living at home. He wanted a change, and he mentioned the possibility of moving to Los Angeles, or New York. He wanted to get away.

Michelle had said that she would miss him if he moved too far away from home, but suggested that he could talk to his Uncle Aiden if he was serious about moving to California. She and his father would help out, but she had agreed to this in a reluctant and exasperated manner.

Perry mentioned that a friend at the restaurant—another waiter named Chip, was considering moving to New York. She warned him that New York was a tough place to live—small apartments, people living on top of each other. He put a piece of cold pizza in the microwave and then told her about the incident at the police station.

Something in her snapped and changed when Perry mentioned that Neal might have a gun—and that her son, after all, could be in danger.

"I don't want you going out of the house till we can go down there and file a complaint," Michelle said. "That man has to be stopped. Did you get the name of who to talk to?"

Perry shook his head, no, then said, "I have to work brunch tomorrow."

"Well, call in sick," she said.

"I can't do that," Perry answered. "I'll lose the job, then I won't have any money to move. The police aren't going to do anything anyway. They don't care. They're on his side."

NINE

Perry slept heavily through the night. In the morning, he went through his usual routine—push-ups, sit-ups, shower, shave, brushing teeth. He listened to a Backstreet Boys CD while he dressed in a clean T-shirt and black slacks, folded the white dress shirt he would put on at the restaurant. The events of the night before seemed distant and surreal. He was calm and thoughtful, without fear or apprehension, but he waited for his parents to leave for church before he went downstairs for breakfast, not wanting a lecture from his mother.

Neal did not have as easy a night. He had stopped at a bar before returning home, chased a few beers with shots of tequila. He wasn't in the mood for the music or the boys preening and camping with the bartender, but he didn't want to drink alone. Around one in the morning, he drove to a convenience store, bought a six pack of beer, and passed out around two in the morning on his couch with the television on. Three hours later he woke up drenched in sweat, his head stuffy and his chest tight. He tried to recall what he'd been watching when he fell asleep but couldn't, and he got up and took an aspirin, then slept in his bed till almost nine.

Before leaving the house, Perry packed his gym bag—replacing a tank top that was smelly with a clean one and tossing in a new pair of socks—he planned to hook up with Will after his shift was done and go to the gym on one of his guest passes. He went on-line and checked his e-mail; there were five spam messages and e-mail from Marcie Stallman, a friend from college who still kept in touch, telling him that she would be in Atlanta in October for a conference. Perry thought about what he would write to his Uncle Aiden if he decided to move to Los Angeles; he had an elaborate dream about how happy he could be in West Hollywood. The words bounced around his head, but he did not type out the note. Instead, he signed off and decided to leave the house as soon as he could, thinking if he left early enough, he could stop by the music store and get the new Alicia Keys CD to listen to at the gym.

It was ten-thirty before Neal felt better and got out of bed. He puttered around the kitchen, made toast and coffee, checked the closing prices of a few stocks, then tried to read an article in the *Journal* he had clipped from the Friday newspaper, but gave up when he couldn't concentrate. The plan came to him while in the shower. He'd go to the gym this morning and work out—that always made him feel better. He'd jog on the treadmill till he couldn't do it anymore, then sit in the steam room. After lunch he'd go to the shooting range and let off a few rounds. Then he'd look for Perry and apologize. While he was still damp from the shower, he dialed Perry's home number and waited for an answer. When the answering machine clicked on, he hung up and dialed The Continental, asking the hostess if Perry was working the brunch shift.

On the drive to work, Perry stopped to gas up the Toyota. The car had 180,000 miles on the meter, but it was reliable and dependable, only the rattle of the glove compartment lock continually irritated Perry, more noticeable when he was listening to a CD than when the stereo was silent. Perry had enough money saved to make a down payment on a new car, but his mother paid for the maintenance and insurance on the Toyota. If she let him have the car, he could stop at the Grand Canyon on his drive cross-country. He wondered if he would need a car in West Hollywood or if he could manage for a while without one. He made a note that it was something else to ask his Uncle Aiden. Before heading out to the restaurant, Perry stopped at the mall and the music store, where he listened to tracks by Rufus Wainwright, Madonna, and Kylie Minogue, before buying new CDs by Macy Gray and Alicia Keys.

At the gym, Neal ran six miles, then worked out with free weights for close to an hour. In the locker room, he used his cell phone to call The Continental and asked to speak with Perry. He waited for a couple of minutes until the hostess returned and said that Perry couldn't come to the phone, did he want to leave a message? Neal knew that Perry was avoiding him and his temperament changed from a combination of frustration and anger. "Tell him not to make any plans after work," Neal said, with a bitterness at the back of his throat. "Or else he's dead."

Brunch was Perry's favorite shift to work. The restaurant was crowded but more polite and relaxed than the Saturday night crowd. The customers were less pressure, not so demanding. He could tell who was hungover, who had slept well, who had scored the night before. Classical musical piped through the sound system instead of the usual bubblegum favorites. If the weather was nice, which it was that afternoon, the windows were open and a breeze ran through the main dining room. There were free refills on Mimosas and Bloody Marys—Claire wandered from table to table with a pitcher refilling glasses, seldom being waved away. Perry flirted with two guys who had obviously hooked up the night before. In back, by the waiter's station, Perry called Will on a break, left a message that he was going to be at his gym later and hoped to see him, maybe do dinner together that evening. He wasn't about to let Neal's threat keep him from doing what he wanted to do.

After the gym, Neal drove to the shooting range out by Stone Mountain. In the car were two pistols—a Smith and Wesson Model 36 and a Colt 38 Special. The Colt had been kept in his office at the restaurant, to use in case of an emergency; he'd been able to keep it out of sight of the bankruptcy liquidators along with a few other personal items. The Smith and Wesson he had kept for security at the house in Jones Mill Estates. In the year he lost his livelihood and filed for divorce, Neal spent the spring at his father's house bewildered and outraged, living in a moldy, damp bedroom above the garage. Once or twice he thought about killing himself, then thought again about shooting his ex-wife or his former business partners who had dragged him into court. To avoid doing either, he had started going to the shooting range to let off steam, finding vindication by personifying his targets, the endorphin rush as beneficial as working out at the gym. He'd avoided mentioning to Perry the guns that he had stored in the back of his closet, not worried that it could alarm his partner, but because it was a forgotten hobby he had neglected while they were still living together. He'd only resumed the practice after Perry moved out and had left him feeling angered and depressed, unable to accept the rejection.

Before his shift was over, Perry told Claire about the late night chase and the incompetence of the county police. It came out sounding too much like a boast, so he teared up his eyes, shook his head of hair, and told her he didn't know what to do. "Somebody should knock that guy out," Claire said, with a sympathetic alliance. She asked Perry if he wanted to go out after their shift was over. He told her about his plans for the gym, adding he needed to shape up, start "looking more like a bully" himself. Then he added that Neal had called the restaurant a few hours ago asking if he was working. "Be on the lookout," he added in a joking manner. "There's sure to be lots of fireworks on the way out."

At the range, Neal fired off two rounds of the Wesson, and six of the Colt. He cleaned the chambers of the Colt, practiced releasing the safety catch, then reloaded the chambers with bullets. On his way out he stopped to talk to Wade Hamden, an ex-cop who worked as a broker at another firm. They talked about a mutual client who was circulating an investment proposal that both of their companies were trying to snare.

Neal asked about Wade's son, who had become a troublesome teen, and after a few remarks, Neal checked his watch and they shook hands and parted.

When his shift ended and Perry had changed his shirt, he exited the kitchen door with Claire and headed toward his car. Outside it was still bright and sunny, just after four o'clock, and he scanned the parking lot to see if he spotted Neal's Jeep, but it was nowhere in sight. They reached Claire's car first—a second-hand baby blue BMW that had once belonged to her older brother—and he kissed her on the cheek and said good-bye, then walked to where the Toyota was parked four spaces away. Inside the car, he buckled the seat belt and put his key in the ignition, noticing in his rear view mirror someone moving through the parking lot. "Shit," he murmured and his stomach became queasy. Neal was walking toward his car. In his hand was a pistol, the silver barrel catching the fading sunlight.

Neal tried to yell to Perry to wait, but his voice caught, paralyzed by fear. He fingered the trigger of the gun, stopped to look down at it and undo the safety catch. He felt his pulse in his ears. There was the dull beginning of a headache that he had chased all day with caffeine and aspirin. With the safety catch off, the gun felt lighter at his side, his grip firmer, even though his palm was sweaty. His arm holding the gun began rising as he grew closer to Perry's car.

Through the mirror Perry could see Neal approaching. Inside the car, the air was stifling hot. Perry inserted the key into the ignition and started up the car. There was a hesitation in the engine, as if the car were unsure how to act in a time of crisis.

Neal reached the Toyota and looked at Perry through the windshield. Perry saw Neal's confused expression. Neal pushed a hand against the window of Perry's car door, tapped it with his knuckles. Then he raised the gun and tapped the tip of it against the glass three times. Click, click, click.

"I warned you," Neal yelled. "Why won't you come back?"

"Go away!" Perry shouted. "Leave me the fuck alone!"

Perry threw the car in reverse and backed out, the car trembling from the surge of gas.

Neal didn't shake as he stepped into the spot the car had vacated, lifted the gun, and aimed at Perry's head, trying to catch Perry's eyes when he turned around. Ungrateful boy, he thought. Never any thanks. Perry was unappreciative of everything Neal had offered him.

Perry turned and saw the gun. He stopped the car with a braking squeal and ducked. Neal straightened his aim and squeezed the trigger.

The window exploded. The glass cracked into a geometrical pattern like the optical ones Perry had studied in a toy kaleidoscope as a boy. The pattern seemed to sigh with breath, turned opaque and shattered apart, the sunlight pouring through a thousand fragments of glass. Perry's expression was a combination of astonishment and pain. Instinctively, his arm went upwards to shield his eyes from the flying shards of glass. The car engine chugged to a stop. Perry felt a burning sensation at his stomach. He pressed his left hand against his shirt and felt the warm sticky gush of blood. He held up a bloody palm toward Neal, tried to say "Why?" but could not make the sound.

Neal took two steps back to avoid the exploding shards, the gun and his arm thrown upward from the discharge. "Why?" Neal yelled. "I warned you. Why?"

Perry's lap was covered with fragments of glass. He scooted quickly across the car seats as though fire were approaching him, aware that he was covered with a sticky film of sweat. Only when he reached for the door handle on the other side did he realize that the blast of the gun had made him momentarily deaf. He opened the car door, rolled his body outside, glass fragments toppling with his arms and legs toward the pavement.

Neal looked down at the gun, touched a finger to the barrel to feel the heat of the discharge, and kept it there, trying to feel the pain. He had watched Perry squirm across the front seat of the car, jiggle the door handle. He raised his arm to aim again, but Perry was crouched too low. He stepped closer to the Toyota, his boots trampling pieces of glass and gravel on the cement.

Perry had landed on his hands and knees. His first thought was that his clothes were ruined. How much would it cost him to buy a new outfit for work? How much would this set him back? There was always a problem with money. He was always relying on the help of his friends. He'd borrowed money from Claire. Will had paid his admission every time they had gone to the movies together. He couldn't ask his parents for more money. Not now. Not while he was wanting to move away.

Neal felt calm now. Level headed. He saw the car. The glass. The curb. The sidewalk. The gardener's wood chips in the nearby flower beds. The air felt thin and it pierced his lungs. He took a deep breath. He was squinting and smiling. He felt like he was finally getting his way.

Perry used the open car door to lift himself off the ground. He saw Neal over the hood of the car. The glare was unrelenting. He was struggling to breathe. He used a hand to wipe his forehead. Neal raised the gun from his side and pointed it at Perry. This time Perry felt the "Why?" rise from his stomach to his throat, but all that came out of his mouth was a breath of confused air.

Neal saw Perry's confusion. The pain. This is what it's been like for me. This is how you've made me feel.

Perry turned away from Neal and took a few steps. He was trying to run. Trying to make one foot go in front of the other. He felt blood pumping in his palms, at his temples, his stomach. He stopped to look at his shirt. There was more blood. Had the bullet hit him here? Or was this from the impact of the glass?

Neal followed, angered that Perry continued to run away. Disgust settled in his throat, his chest tightened. He gripped the Colt 38 tighter. Sweat rivered beneath his arms, the pressure of his pulse made his field of vision throb. He raised the gun and shot Perry in the back. Once, twice, and then a third time. The shots echoed off the hot metal of the cars. Boom. Boom. *Boom.*

Perry felt his foot rise from the ground and fall; his hands clenched into fists as he used his arms to move faster. He heard the bullet before he felt the sting below his left shoulder. It was like an insect bite that grew into an itchy rash that turned into a merciless punch that knocked the wind out of his lungs. He wobbled as though he were a drunk, forced to walk a straight line at midnight in a small town. Sound fell away again, all except the scrape of the bottom of his shoes against the cement surface of the parking lot. But then the silence was followed by the sound of more bullets, though this time he didn't feel the sting of them. When the third bullet hit, he had lifted his foot high enough to make it over the curb of the parking lot and reach the edge of a bed of grass along the sidewalk. He thought that if he made it back to the restaurant he would be free of Neal. That this would all be a mistake, an illusion, a nightmare. And he would be safe.

Claire had seen the car window shatter, the chase across the parking lot, the gun shots enter Perry's back, Neal's final bullet entering the back of Perry's head. She had slowly pulled herself out of her car, yelled at Neal, "Are you crazy? What the hell are you doing?"

Neal watched Claire run across the black pavement toward the kitchen door of the restaurant, the details of the afternoon and the landscape sharpening in his mind as he watched her progress: the swirl of the pattern of stucco waterproofing that partially covered the old red bricks at the back of the building, the hanging baskets of white geraniums in the opened windows, the bright white cotton shirt of an overweight man at the side entrance of the restaurant as he turned at the sounds behind him in the parking lot, flattening his palm against his forehead to shield the glare and look at Perry only yards away. Neal felt certain that this was what he had wanted, no doubt that this was the right and natural path to take. His self-confidence restored, he lifted the gun to his temple and fired.

Neal felt the sound of the trigger at his ear. There was a blinding light and his hand was pushed away with the force of the bullet. The gun dropped to the ground with a clackety echo that was lost in disbelief. The bullet traveled through Neal's skull and came to rest in the black cement twenty-one feet away.

Then there was nothing, the misery finally over for two men, but just beginning for others.

TEN

I did not hear of Neal's death until almost a year and a half later. The news of the murder and suicide did not carry beyond the local Georgia press, except in a few scattered gay newspapers, none of which I saw at the time. Instead, I was consumed with matters of my own in Manhattan. I was forty-five that year, had lived in Manhattan for twenty-three years. I had had a successful business career, owned a nice one-bedroom apartment in the West Village, but for more than I could remember I had bounced from one short-term boyfriend to another, never able to make it beyond a six-month commitment with a guy, a portion of which I will accept blame for but not all. By then, early September of 2001, I'd reached an age where I was comfortable with being a single man who could still find himself prone to the restless yearnings of desiring a partnered existence if he met the right man. The Saturday night Neal chased Perry's car down the Atlanta Interstate, I had been out on a date with Brice, a man I had been dating sporadically for almost nine weeks, and with whom I had developed a casual, but seriously growing relationship. The following morning, Sunday, I woke up in Brice's small studio on the west side of midtown in the lower 50s. It was a sparsely furnished room with only a sofa-bed, kitchen table, and chairs. There was a framed photo of a floating red apple on one of the walls—one of those surreal kinds of posters that seem more at home in a college dorm than in the living quarters of a professional businessman. The toiletries in the bathroom cabinet were minimal—toothbrush, razor, deodorant—certainly not the kind of clutter of colognes and medications of a settled-in fortysomething-year-old man. But then I knew that Brice had not lived here long; the night we met he had confessed leaving behind a long-term relationship with someone in New Jersey.

Brice was two inches taller than me and three years younger, and I had been attracted to him by his wicked smile the night I met him in a Village bar. Raised in the suburbs of New Jersey, he worked downtown as a lawyer for a commodities trading firm, and there was something of a bad boy character to him that he had not shaken in adulthood—as if his pockets were full of firecrackers and matches, but perhaps of an altogether different kind. Undressed he displayed a whiff of arrogance, proud of his smooth chest, his hairy forearms, and the thicker forest at his groin. In bed with him that night, he took charge of everything—spreading my legs, reaching for lube, keeping himself deep inside me until I would wince and have to shift—all of which I wanted and needed at that moment in my life—someone to keep me guessing and engaged, someone who might penetrate me and wrench me into a change.

By my estimation Brice was my 267th sexual partner since moving to Manhattan at the age of twenty-one, just out of college. For a sexually-active, single gay man in search of a longtime companion, I'd always considered this a conservative number when compared to other unpartnered gay men of my generation; I was not one for anonymous encounters—I wanted to know my partner's name, his details, the facts of his life in order to imagine myself becoming a part of it. I'd always approached sex as a potential introductory service, a way to find a boyfriend, as it were, and Brice was no different than any other man for me in this regard. We spent the following morning—Sunday—the day Neal shot Perry—watching the political commentary shows on television and cooking breakfast, and in the early afternoon took a walk to Central

126

Park where we parted later; he back to his place, me to attend an off-off-Broadway showcase performance of a woman who worked at my office (and which I had promised to spare Brice the misery of watching her mangle standard cabaret tunes).

The following day, Monday, I had congratulated Reyna, my office assistant, on her cabaret performance, attended a meeting for a client, and went straight home after work with a minor sinus headache, and again, I would have had no reason to access any news from Atlanta, so was spared knowing the details of the killings, the reports delivered by on-the-scene local television journalists. Nor did I speak with Brice that evening—before parting on Sunday we had made plans to get together again on Friday, perhaps renting a car and spending the weekend in New Hope and Bucks County, and we had agreed to talk later in the week. That night, it rained miserably in the evening, the water splattering against the window as if being thrown from the sky in buckets, and I spent a good deal of time fretting over a growing wet spot at the ceiling of my kitchen and how I would inform the co-op board of the problem, then had a few beers and fallen asleep on the couch watching TV.

The next morning was the kind of perfect weather that makes Manhattan so tolerable during its more miserable days of the year—the sun was bright, the air was cool and clear. From the window of my bedroom I could see the sunlight catching windows on the Jersey side of the Hudson River. I heard the first siren as I was getting out of the subway at 53rd and Third and walking down toward the building where I worked, but I still did not sense anything unusual about the day. By the time I reached my office the first plane had already hit the North Tower of the World Trade Center. A receptionist handed me a message from the day before and then said that the Trade Center had been "bombed," which was the information she had gotten that moment from a co-worker. When I reached my desk, there were several people rushing through the hallway outside my office to a television set which was kept in a nearby conference room. It took me a few seconds after I turned on my computer to remember that Brice had said that he worked at the Trade Center, but I had no recollection of the name of his firm or whether he was in the North or South tower—or if he had even given me that information. All I could recollect was that he was proud of the view from his office—he could see the Statue of Liberty if he swiveled his chair.

A few minutes later when I walked into the conference room, the second plane hit the South Tower, and I realized I had no office phone number for Brice, nor a cell phone number—only his home phone number. I walked back to my office and dialed his apartment and left a message: "Brice, it's Tom. Please call me and let me know you're all right." I left my office number, my home number, and my cell phone number and expected the phone to ring as soon as I placed the receiver in the cradle. It did, of course, but it was not Brice, but my sister Allison in West Virginia asking if I was all right—she had just seen a news bulletin on television. From my desk I heard the gasps of co-workers when the South Tower collapsed, and I hung up from my sister and returned to the conference room, watched the news reports, then saw the North Tower collapse a few minutes later.

I went back to my office and checked my voice mail, my home answering machine, and the battery of my cell phone. Brice had not called, nor had I really expected to hear from him so quickly. Sometime after noon I left the office and walked west along 42nd Street toward the Hudson River. Above the buildings to the south, smoke was drifting over the water in two grayish funnels, the sky continued to be strangely bright blue and clear around them because there was only a little breeze to the day, though there was already a strange, bitter stench in the air. I stayed at the waterfront until early evening watching the smoke drift over the river, the ambulances and police cars and fire trucks speed along the West Side Highway, and reached a co-worker Ed and his lover David on my cell phone who met me at the entrance to the piers at the end of Christopher Street for a few minutes, then I walked to my apartment and spent the evening watching the news.

My parents reached me at home, as did my older brother and my youngest sister. Scott called me from Los Angeles to make sure I was all right, and we had a brief conversation about his new boyfriend Aiden who was in Atlanta to attend his nephew's funeral. He told me a little of the details of the murder in a few gruesome asides, none of which I had any reason to connect with Neal, and I let out an "Oh my gosh," and "You're serious?" until we returned to my describing the pallor that now hung over Manhattan. I didn't mention anything to Scott about my fear that Brice might have been a part of the tragedy—I hadn't even told Scott that I was dating anyone seriously, not wanting to give Brice that kind of depth in my life, fearing, and just knowing instinctively, that I would soon have to let go and find closure instead.

Brice did not call that day, or that night, or the next morning. The whole time my television set remained on while I listened to one gruesome fact after the next—the estimation of the casualties, the hijacked passengers, office workers jumping from windows on the upper floors because of the high temperature of the fire, the firemen climbing the stairwells only to meet their inevitable end in the collapse. Brice did not live in a doorman building so there was no way for me to easily find out if he had returned to his apartment unless I waited for a neighbor outside and asked them to check— and my avoidance of doing that seemed to subconsciously confirm what I already suspected. Instead, I made my way to where other New Yorkers were gathering for news, outside St. Vincent's Hospital, only a few blocks from my apartment, where an eerily quiet and respectful crowd of people had assembled. Again, the weather was beautiful, the sky high and baby blue, though the wind had shifted and the bitter stench hung all around us now—or perhaps my notice of it had been magnified because of what I suspected it was. I was also aware that I had survived something others had not. Not once, but twice. AIDS. And now this. When a woman weaved through the crowd handing each of us a flyer with a picture of her husband who was missing, I realized then what little memories and possessions I had of Brice, though I was certain of what I missed. The rush of grief that I had successfully come to terms with year after year of watching lovers and friends die from the epidemic came tumbling back into my consciousness.

I remembered this moment, this weight of Brice and Kyle and Jeff and Paul and Tony and all the others, when Aiden explained that his nephew's funeral was the morning of 9/11. We were all in the Great Room again; Harley and Scott's eyelids were heavy, watching the fire flicker and rise. Zero had collapsed onto his side, his ribcage rising and falling with his sleeping breaths. I had been looking at the deep blue of the night at the window, not following the conversation as closely as I should have. Aiden was nursing the last third of his after-dinner drink and some of his words were thick and slurry, his shoulders hunched forward from the weight of grief. "We were still trying to get as many details as we could about what had happened between Neal and Perry and then it was like the program had been turned off, pre-empted by another, larger tragedy."

Scott's eyes drifted from the fire toward mine; he knew of my involvement with Brice and its outcome, though I had no idea if he had confided it to Aiden and Aiden did not act as if he had been told. I had never told Harley of Brice, however, telling him that my catalyst for leaving New York was simply a need for change after so many years in Manhattan. I had told him of Kyle's death, of Paul's and Tony's long illnesses, and my bittersweet book of eulogies becoming a novel, but I had kept my short affair with Brice a secret from him because it was the sharpest and most perceptible pain I had experienced in the months before I met him and I was concerned that it might reveal me to be a too vulnerable and unsteady man, particularly since he had sought me out to help himself become more balanced. It had been so much easier to unemotionally write the news of what had happened in an e-mail to Scott than it had been to try to summon up the courage to describe the confusion of the events of Brice to Harley face-to-face. Now I had buried as much as I could of the memory of Brice, just as I had done with Mitch years before.

In the days following the collapse of the Towers, I learned through a neighbor that Brice had not returned to his apartment. (I had finally reached someone whose name I had copied down from the buzzers beside the door of his building and found in the phone book.) Each morning I awoke hearing explosions and sirens outside my apartment and felt uncertain how to start the day—Should I go to work? Should I remain home? Should I try and get out of the city? Fighter planes could be heard flying across the sky above the buildings. Even before my body had fully awakened I turned on the TV expecting a worse turn of events. The news would greet me that no one was rescued, that any survivor might have been pulverized in the collapse of the buildings, and that the wind had shifted and the strange smell I now detected in my apartment was the aftermath of the burning buildings and lost victims. "Life would never be the same," every newscaster and commentator predicted. I continued to wander through the empty streets of the city, finding my way to the gathering points at Union Square and the Armory on Lexington Avenue, where there were others who wanted to find news of the missing. All the while I expected that there was someone else who wanted to know exactly what I was after, that someone would hand me a flyer with Brice's photo on it, and I would call the number, find a connection with a friend or family member, and learn the story of who he really was.

Instead, Brice's death was confirmed by a short profile in a newspaper. Forty-six days after the Towers fell, there was his photo and a small description of who he was: "He was a good-time guy," said his wife Janice. They met in a bar in Asbury Park. "I went there with my sister and he just caught my eye with his blue eyes and big smile," she said. "I always say we met through my sister and he would say we met in a bar."

Brice was not even the man I had imagined him to be and I felt both saddened and disturbed by what little new details of him was here—he had no reason to tell me he was recently separated from his wife—or did he? There was only "someone he had left behind." I obviously had not turned the corner of becoming someone special in his life to have learned even this much about him. He had never mentioned to me that he was also the father of a nine-year-old daughter and a five-year-old son. Danie. And Jesse. The following day after the newspaper had confirmed everything I had suspected, I came down with the flu and stayed away from work the rest of the week. I writhed and sweated and burned Brice out of my body, day by day by day by day, even though I knew he did not consider me as seriously as I now considered him. Sometime in December, I reached a closure on the aborted relationship and Brice's unknown past by deciding it was time for me to leave New York. It was April of the next year by the time I sold my apartment, weeded through my books and papers, and used my savings and the income from the sale of the apartment to put a down payment on a building in Asheville that housed a print shop and where I took an apartment on the top floor. In another unfortunate turn of events, the firm in Manhattan was glad to see me resign—a downturn in revenues in the wake of 9/11 was forcing management into layoffs. I was able to escape Manhattan with a buyout and my pension intact.

"I ended up staying in Atlanta for almost two weeks," Aiden said. "Not because I was afraid to fly back to Los Angeles, but because Michelle was so depressed she couldn't even cook. There was just no way to get around the bigger issue of the attacks. She accused the police department of homophobia and there was no response from them, because they were suddenly more concerned with terrorism. Dave wanted to sue the restaurant owner, the police departments, and the city, counties, and state because no one did anything that could have helped Perry, but he couldn't get a meeting with a lawyer—everyone was staying home. I tried to be as supportive as I could, but I felt in the way. Michelle would keep walking into Perry's bedroom, as if expecting to find him there. She still has his contact solution and shaving cream in the bathroom cabinet. His clothes are still hanging in the closet. She's turned his bedroom into a shrine."

"All they talked about during Thanksgiving dinner were the court cases they are filing," Scott said. "One procedure after the next. You'd think they were lawyers now with how much they know about the law."

"They'll be in court for years," Aiden said. "It's rather empowering to see all that they know about due process now and appeals and lawsuits. And what they are doing to try to change the laws, particularly in gay domestic abuse situations and how the police respond to them—even in a conservative state like Georgia. But all they really want is someone to admit that there was something more that someone could have done to help Perry. To keep Neal away from him. They'd drop all the lawsuits if the policies were put in place or someone said 'I'm sorry. We were responsible for this.'"

Aiden finished the last of his drink and said, "I'm as bad as she is. Talking about him for so long. I'm counting on you to distract us tomorrow. We're looking forward to seeing all the big hot spots of Asheville. Do some shopping. I hope it'll be a nice day."

Harley told them the forecast for the weather, and I asked them if they had brought enough warm clothing as we gathered up the drinks and brought them into the kitchen. I mentioned where they could find an extra blanket in the guest room, if it turned too cold and was needed, and then offered to get them a final drink.

"I shouldn't," Aiden said, rolling his eyes.

"But he will," Scott answered with a long nod of his head. "In fact, we'll both take something back to the bedroom with us. Keep us from pretending the other one is still there."

ELEVEN

In the bedroom, the curtains were open and outside the floodlight on the side of the house cast both light and shadows across the deck until Harley flipped the switch off in the kitchen. I thought for a moment about turning on the television, but was grateful for the absence of sound and the news. As I unbuttoned the shirt I had been wearing, I walked to the closet and hung it on a hook and pulled on a sweatshirt for warmth. Ever since I was a boy I'd suffered from poor circulation; even in the warmest of weather I slept in socks to keep my feet warm, and tonight as I slipped off my jeans, I slipped on an old pair of sweat pants to sleep in and checked the thermostat on the wall.

Harley walked into the room and pulled the sweater he had been wearing over his head, tossed it on the seat of a chair, sat down on the bed and unlaced his boots. One after the other, he threw the boots to the other side of the room to a corner near the closet, his usual method of undressing. The clump-clump of the boots woke Zero in the other room, and he padded into the bedroom, looked at both of us, walked to Harley's boots and sniffed them.

Harley unzipped his jeans, lifting his legs to pull the pants off. The jeans were tossed on top of the sweater and for a few moments we went about our activities getting ready for bed, lost in our own thoughts as we brushed our teeth, pissed and flushed, washed the film from the fireplace and the cooking from our faces. Zero jumped up on the bed and collapsed on his side in his usual place. At one point Harley stood and placed his hands on his hips, his gaze fastened out onto the dark deck outside our bedroom as if he were waiting for the light to come on and cast something suspicious into view. I asked him, "Are you tired?"

He turned away from the window slowly and walked in front of the lamp beside the bed. His face looked serious and weary.

"A bit," he answered.

"You're not getting sick, are you?" I asked him; ill health was always at the tip of my fears and I was forever thinking of ways to keep from getting sicker—herbal tea, more fruit and roughage, an aspirin for prevention.

"No, just ate too much."

I was pulling the comforter and sheets back away from the pillows and he approached me from behind and wrapped his arms around my waist, lifting my body slightly from the floor and nuzzling his neck against mine. I broke into a smile from the crush of him as he pulled me up and close to him.

"You know how much you mean to me," he said. "You know how much I need this."

From any other lover I would have found those kind of words patronizing, a prelude to the "but ifs" of ending a relationship. Nonetheless, it signaled to me that there was something on Harley's mind which he wanted to disclose. I turned my body around in his embrace and my arms reached around his body and found the rise of his buttocks. I slipped my fingers beneath the waistband of his boxers in a teasing sort of way, nodding my forehead against his bare chest and nuzzling my lips against his skin, drawing in the smell of him to resist my own urge to begin asking questions and hoping we might fall into sex instead.

Harley tilted back from me, took a few steps back so that he could catch my eyes. As soon as he caught my gaze, he deflected his own eyes to his bare knees and he walked to the bureau and found a clean T-shirt and slipped it on. I watched him do this, then settled myself in bed. I knew something was on his mind and that he was not really in the mood for sex, but instead of waiting for him to find the courage to bring up whatever it was he needed to tell me, I finally asked him, "What's wrong?"

"I don't know what I would do if I lost you right now," he said, after a few seconds of thought. "I want you to know how thankful I am for all this."

The truth was I did not know what I could do without Harley. This house would mean nothing without him. Without his endless projects it would feel empty, as would I. I needed him to keep going because it kept us going, kept me going in what felt like the right direction. Without him, I would only be likely to stop and give up, fall again into a dark depression. I doubt that I could stay here, all alone except for the dogs, outside of town in a rural, conservative pocket of the world. I would end up giving the dogs away, selling the cabin, perhaps even return to Manhattan where I could be lonely, even though I was not alone, surrounded by the traffic and tourists and workers who made it seem as if I were still a part of it all, even though I wasn't.

My eyes moved away from him, out to the room where one boot stood upright on the floor, the other lay twisted on its side. My mind drifted to the hours before and our dinner and the interweaving trails of Neal and Perry. Was Harley going to tell me that I should not have started it, talking about Neal, egging Aiden on to talk about Perry? But Harley had also wanted to hear the story as much as I did, perhaps because I had told him so little of it myself. It was the reason why I had invited our guests for the weekend, after all; I wanted to lay all the pieces together and convince myself that Neal was not a killer. Now my own memory seemed so foolish and young and distant and Aiden's bitterness logical and deserved. Neal was not at all the man I had known. Or was he?

I leaned my head against the headboard and said, "What are you thinking about?"

He did not answer, but stood with his back to me, his eyes cast out into the dark valley, so I asked, again, "Is something wrong?"

He let out a sigh and turned his head toward me, over his shoulder, his eyes cast toward the ceiling. "I never told you about Chris," he said.

I caught sight of Harley's reflection in the window, the baggy shape of the T-shirt and boxers, the darkness of his legs disappearing into the background of the night. There were plenty of things in our past we did not know of each other, plenty of men and women and boyfriends and girlfriends and ex-lovers, but we had never let them interfere with what we had now. "Did you want to talk about it?"

He walked to the door and turned off the overhead light and the room was cast into the glow from the bedside lamps. At the door he said, "I wasn't such a nice guy."

"What happened?"

"I'd just broken up with him—the first time we met," he said.

"The time you were so drunk."

"He was a young guy," Harley said. He leaned against the wall, wanting—or needing—to keep a distance between us. "College kid. I wasn't very nice when he wanted to end it. I was crazy about him. Couldn't get enough of him. It was very sexual. Which also made it very emotional for me. But it wasn't just great sex. We did a lot of things together, too. I thought of him as a friend. Which made him a better lover for me."

"How long did it go on?"

"The affair?" Harley answered. "About six months. Long enough for me to leave Geena and start caring about him."

Harley cleared his throat and I could tell he was holding something back and his next sentence arrived in a bitter flush of words. "I gave up so much."

Geena was Harley's wife; they had been high school sweethearts, marrying each other when they were both eighteen. Gillian, their oldest child, had married and now lived in Greensboro, and Rob, their younger son, had enlisted in the army after graduating high school. Harley had once told me that he always knew he would leave Geena one day, but I can imagine the difficulty he must have had in telling her why. "You were in love with him?" I asked.

"I met him when his car broke down. It was during the end of his junior year. The winter was really bad. He had an old Saab. It broke down while he was trying to get back from Atlanta. Late at night. He'd gone to a club—I didn't know that then—when I met him. I was on duty that night and I got the call to go out to I-26 and tow back his car. When I got there he said he was low on money and didn't have much more coming in. He asked if he could barter something for the help—he offered to give me a blow job for the tow."

Harley bowed his head and smiled and I let out a short, disbelieving laugh; it was the type of scenario you would expect to find in a porn film—college student stranded, no money, big hunky mechanic arrives to save the day. I could imagine Harley's surprise at the offer though I could not believe that it was the first of the kind he had ever received. "And so you let him . . . ," I said, part statement, part question, and waited for him to continue.

Harley nodded and his smile became a boyishly crooked grin. "He was cute. He was younger than my son. What did I have to lose? I could fudge the paperwork some. He was in school at UNC, so I drove him back to the campus, then took his car in. When the car was repaired and ready to be picked up, I drove it out to his dorm, got another blow job, and asked him if he wanted to go out to the movies and get something to eat. That started things up. I never expected it to go so far. I didn't think it would turn out as it did."

In my mind I had an image of Harley freshly showered and nicely dressed, patiently waiting by his truck at the corner of a parking lot. His expression changes as his young man finds him, only it isn't Chris in my imagination, it's the Jeff of my college days. I imagine Harley's eagerness and Jeff's recklessness together and I only see trouble headed for one of them. One of them would not be able to shake off the impression of the other, and I knew from my past that it would not be Jeff.

"He wanted to live together during summer break, so that's when I left Geena," Harley said. "I thought he was serious about making it work. Staying together. We got a cheap place that had a tiny kitchen. We spent a lot of time together because of my odd hours—going to the movies in the afternoon, coming back having sex before I went out to work. Then all of a sudden he wanted to break up when school started back again because he wanted to live in the dorm."

"What did you do to him?"

"Nothing to him," Harley said. "I couldn't hurt him. "I threw all his clothes out into the parking lot one night. And then I totaled his car, just sent it into the ditch while I jumped out of it. I thought that might keep him around a bit longer—if he needed me to drive him places, and if he stayed a bit longer, then he wouldn't want to leave because I wanted to make things work out."

"And did he? Leave?"

"He left," Harley said. "I told him his car had been stolen. I know he guessed that it was me who did it, but he never confronted me on it. His parents' insurance covered it. I went to his dorm a few weeks later, tracked him down outside one of his classes. I told him he was a prick and he would regret doing this. I was upset. Hurt. He dumped me. He wasn't dumping me for someone else. There wasn't anybody else to be jealous of. He was just dumping me to move back to school. He'd just used me to mark time. I didn't ever want to feel like that again. In love. Or out of it. It was just a miserable feeling. I didn't want to kill him. But I wanted to kill myself. The campus police picked me up a few minutes later on the way back to my truck. One of Chris's friends had called 9-1-1 on his cell phone because he

140

thought I was going to hurt Chris. He didn't file any charges and there was no record of it, but I signed a release form that if I ever showed up on campus again I would be arrested."

"Was that legal?" I asked. "Could they do that?"

"I don't know," he said. "I didn't want to go back there again anyway. I was ashamed of my behavior. Things got bad after that. I started drinking a lot more. Got real depressed. That's when I first met you. After that incident."

"Did you hurt him?"

"No," Harley said. "But I could have."

"But you didn't," I said "You didn't do it."

"No," he answered me. "But I'm so much like him. Your friend. Neal."

"You're not," I answered. "You're different."

"I wanted to kill myself," Harley said.

I'd reached the end of that rope, too. When Kyle died. When I buried Paul. When things with Jeff and Russell and Bill and Mitch did not work out. When the Towers fell and I discovered that Brice was married. "But you didn't," I said.

"No," he answered. "I didn't."

"We've all felt like that sometime." I said. "We've all been in that place, once or twice."

TWELVE

"Will you write about this?" Glenn asked. His lips were against my neck and his words were whispers, soft pulses of breath and sound.

I smiled and angled my body across the bed so that I could see his face beside me. "Should I be taking notes?" I answered.

His eyes were boyish and mischievous, but his face was darkly handsome and masculine. "I've never slept with an author before," he said.

"Neither have I," I answered.

I seldom admitted that I was a writer, in truth, because it was an avocation and not my profession, but that night when I had walked through the East Village and stopped at a bar for a drink, I wanted to be someone else. Someone taller, younger, better-looking, happier than whom I was at that moment. I was forty-one years old that year and had just reached the end of another relationship; Russell, the guy I had been dating for four months, had called that afternoon to cancel our date and bluntly admit it was over, it wasn't working out for him, and I had not had the enthusiasm to try and persuade him otherwise because I felt the same. Sitting next to Glenn at the bar, we had lobbed questions at each other until we introduced ourselves and I disclosed that I had once written and published a book, in order not to confess my recent break-up with Russell.

"How would you describe my best feature?" Glenn asked me hours later, rolling back on his knees so that he towered above me, his stomach flexed flat, his ass as hard and round as a basketball, his cock and balls dangling and swinging between his thighs.

I have not thought of Glenn for many years, but I see him quite clearly as a memory tonight, seven years later, as I pull myself out of bed and away from Harley. Harley was sleeping, curled on his side, his arms snaking around my waist, and once out of bed, I leaned back down and settled the blanket around his chest to replace the warmth his body would miss from my own. Zero's eyes popped open and he lifted his head toward me in his curious way and I patted him back down to sleep and gingerly picked my way through the room. Glenn was just a one-night stand, but his question had stirred something in me both then and now. Then, I had answered him with a laugh, watched him swing his long, narrow cock back and forth in a taunting, egotistical way, and reached for a small towel I kept nearby to wipe away our come and sweat. Could I write about him? I had considered after Glenn left my apartment after a quick shower. Physically, I felt with him the promise of what a lover could be—both good and bad—the pain and pleasure of our joined bodies could easily be described. Emotionally, it was a more complicated story—my mind was thick, full of history and hopes, half-remembered, half-forgotten, yet hungry, full of a great thirst to feel connected to someone, something that I did not wish to publicly release by writing it down. I could make the character of Glenn distinct, of course; I could give him specific physical features and a definitive personality, but my imagined future with him had been no different from any of my other sexual partners. I wanted him to be something more than he was at that moment he was inside of me. Could I write that right? Or would that desire seem repetitive, an idyllic pursuit?

What does that say about me now that his question still rattled me and sent me about the rooms of the cabin all these years later? *Will you write about this?* At the time, I had no interest in writing about Glenn, though I can recall the trivial details of him very well: the mole on the left side of his chest, the overlapping front teeth, the earthy smell of his groin. He was simply another man who came and went through my bedroom in the hopes of finding a long-term lover. But now, years later, he was some kind of ghostly guide drawing me out of bed, a crucial tool I clutched at and carried in my mind in order to begin writing again, to want to seek out the definitive moment of another story, a way to look inside what it meant for me to write, to set down not only the facts and details, but an understanding of why they were there, why they were important to me. As I stood in the quiet darkness of the bedroom watching Harley and Zero sleep, I realized I never consciously stopped writing, nor did I run out of things to write. I found other ways to deal with my inner demons, that troublesome part of my brain always looking for rational explanations and which led me to the sit down in front of the keyboard in the first place. But solitude can be a dangerous narcotic; now there were secrets haunting me which I wanted to release, wanted Harley to know of and thought it might be best if he came to them this way, on paper, in a story. Writing cannot heal an infected soul, nor can it return what has already been lost, but I could use it as my advocate to help explain my facts, hope that it could provide a deeper connection with my new lover.

This is what makes the writing different, I thought, cautiously stepping through the darkened Great Room, around the chairs which had not been tucked neatly under the dining room table, around the snout of the bear-skinned rug, the smoky smell of the wood from the fireplace as thick as the room was black. I knew Neal before he was a murderer, before he killed himself. Was there something in the history of our friendship that could lead me into seeing the man he became? Did I perhaps play a part in this—knowingly or unknowingly? Could I use this story to reveal things on paper that I had avoided speaking about face-to-face to Harley? A reviewer once said that I could write beautiful elegies because I had never really loved a man, that I was emotionally disconnected, unable to commit to just one guy, regarding all of them, instead, as interesting paintings I might admire in a museum. It was amazing how such a comment could wound me. Was this why I had stopped writing? Could I not connect with one man? Did I fail because I had sequestered my emotions to keep myself strong? Was this why I harbored secrets from Harley, afraid of frightening him away with revelations of my past? Or was there something else that I had buried away long ago in my memory that I needed to find again?

Standing in front of the computer, I switched on the power; the eerie light from the monitor glowed bright enough to cast my reflection against the window. Outside, the driveway and mountains were absent, and my reflection was nothing but a featureless shape, though a new demon has found its way inside of me and was ready to escape. Beside me on the desk were the photos which were always there—me with my parents when I was eight, my sister's wedding party when I was thirty-one, myself and Kyle on the beach at Atlantic City when we were both twenty-six. I lifted the photo from college which had first caught Aiden's eye. I was nineteen years old and my smile was genuine, full of happiness and hope of a young man without an ounce of discouragement. The day I had found an account on the killings on the Internet in the archive of a gay news service and read about the events of Neal and Perry, I had thought that the reporter must have confused the facts. Neal could not have killed someone, nor could he have reached that level of despair to make him want to take his own life. But if the random quirks and disappointments of life had beaten and changed him as it had so many of us, could this have been his response? I searched for more information and found another article at a different news site and on the right side of the screen were photos of both Neal and Perry. Perry's similarity to how I looked in college was a shocking recognition to arrive at and I knew when Aiden had picked up the photo earlier in the day, he must have thought the same. What part could I have played in Neal taking his own life? In killing Perry? Was there some memory of him that I had hidden away along with my secrets of Mitch and Brice?

In the photograph, there was a light blur to Jeff's face as he stepped to the foreground trying to shield his expression from the camera lens with his hand. Jeff and I had slipped away from Neal while we were in a card store that afternoon in Asheville, walked down the street and gotten sodas from a vending machine at the side of a garage. I can also recall these details with vivid clarity: the light breaking through the leaves of the trees on the other side of the street, the backfire of a car's muffler that made us startle and giggle, the sparkle of mica chips in the cement of the sidewalks at our feet. I realized that afternoon that Jeff had released a dangerous joy in me. We had stood in the sun drinking the sodas, the cold carbonation burning our throats and tearing our eyes. We were both obnoxious and dauntless as we stood close to each other, drawn in by the other's aura and not willing to break orbits. He had never seemed more handsome or more special to me than at that moment and I felt myself willing to follow him wherever he wanted to lead me, like an inner tube thrust into the currents of a river, never questioning or panicking over the rushing direction or the stony, jagged path it might take.

Neal had found us sometime later when we were looking at the menu in the window of a restaurant and he had rushed toward us with his camera. Jeff noticed him approaching and raised his hand toward his face in a defensive but playful "Stop! No pictures!" Neal had always been running to catch up with us. "Why didn't you guys wait for me?" he would ask when we would leave choral rehearsals without him to walk back to the dorm, or if he discovered us later, climbing the stairs to our rooms after watching a film together at the student center. In truth it became a sort of boyish game Jeff and I would play, a prankish "let's ditch Neal," or "let's leave before he can find us," and it became an affectionate way we bonded stronger with each other, as well as being a gentle manner of teasing and torturing Neal. Neal never seemed annoyed by our behavior, or so I thought, and that weekend in Asheville twenty-nine years ago he had used the camera as a weapon, trying to catch us off guard, to take a bad, unflattering snapshot in order to get back at us for deserting him. I'd always felt it was an immature reaction, as mischievous as our own hide-and-seek strategy. Could this chase that we had initiated all those years earlier have subconsciously inspired Neal's more frantic pursuit of Perry?

Will you write about this? Glenn had asked me and if I were to write about him now, just him, our evening together, I would describe it as a black and white experience. A one night stand. He was nothing more. Or less. Some fun, a recreational moment, a man I liked but did not expect anything else further from, even with all of my emotional subtext thrown in. If I were to write about Jeff or Kyle I would say they were Technicolor, and that I missed them both deeply, though in different, aching ways. But in truth, I feel that every man I'd ever had sex with has made me recognize something about myself: who I am, what I fear, what arouses me in bed, what I desire once the orgasm is done.

When I first read of the killings I had a series of images of Neal rise up at me, like a collage of pictures used in a movie depicting a rapid passage of time: there he was at the side of the stage of *Rosencrantz*, watching me mangle my lines; there he was again, a little older, pushing the door open of my Village apartment, his eyes puffy from his all-night escapade at a sex club. And there he was again, thin and handsome in his tuxedo beneath the white tenting of his wedding stage.

But what must you write about this? Glenn's ghost prodded me as the computer software opened to a blank page and I sat in the chair at the desk, the cursor on the monitor screen blinking in front of my eyes, waiting, waiting, waiting. *What is the story you feel you must tell now? What are you keeping*

buried, hidden deep, deep inside that you want to let go of?
What will let you connect deeper?

I began to type:

This is the truth about Neal. The story of what happened one night between us. It was the last days of our spring semester, our sophomore year, not long after our trip to Asheville. My four finals had been separated by days, a waiting period from one test to the next. My roommate had finished his exams the first day and Jeff had had the luck (or misfortune, depending on how you looked at it) of having all of his tests occur in a short, but brutal, two-day period. At the end of them he had packed up his belongings and flown back to his mother's house in Maryland where he would spend the summer. I was still in the dorm, waiting for the final day and my final test. Neal was there as well, though many of the other students had already left campus—few of us ever had finals on the last day of the testing period.

I had returned from the library and thrown my books and notebooks on my bed, slipped out of my jeans and T-shirt, draped a towel around my waist and headed down to the showers, which were in a communal bathing facility off the center of the hallway. It was late at night and it was a hot, muggy June day; the dorms were not air-conditioned and I was trying to find a way to stay awake a few more hours in order to cram for a course I did not much like. As I passed Neal's room, I saw that his door was shut and the light was off inside his room.

In the bathroom, I hung my towel on a hook outside the shower stalls and padded my way toward the one which I always felt was the cleanest and had the best water pressure. I turned on the spigots, stepped into the stream of warm water and showered, shampooed my hair, and dried off with my towel. I was combing my hair at the sink when I saw Neal enter the bathroom through the misty reflection of the mirror. Like me, he wore only a towel and had a pair of flip-flops on his feet, and he came over to where I stood at the sink and mirrors and began asking how my studying was going.

"You must be tired," he said, after I had finished complaining about the time I had spent worrying over the translation of a Latin passage in a book.

"Not too," I answered, turning to face him. I noticed that Neal had not brought any toiletries into the bathroom with him, but I thought he must have just returned from studying at the library as I had and was probably rinsing off to cool down from the heat of the day and the stuffiness of the dorm rooms.

He took a step closer toward me and stretched his hand out toward the wall. "You want to feel better?" he asked, angling his body so that he locked me into position against the sink, his free hand slipping under my towel and finding my cock.

I stood there astonished by his aggressiveness. He had never directed such a sexual interest toward me, nor had he acted so physically assertive. As for myself, I had not reached a comfortable resolution or acceptance of my own homosexuality and I allowed his hand to remain on my cock long enough to become worried by the rising reaction of it.

"Let's not," I said and pulled myself away from him so that his hand left my cock and fell against my thigh. I turned myself partially around and made a move to slip under his outstretched arm, when he used the movement to grasp me from behind. Again his hand returned to my cock and he stroked it once or twice, his other arm pinning me across the chest, his palm flattening against my stomach. The towel fell away from my waist and I struggled to get out of his hold. He grasped me tighter, seemed pleased by my struggle, till I squirmed and poked him in the ribs with my elbow and he understood that my reaction was not a playful one. I pushed myself away from him and squatted down to the floor to retrieve my towel. He towered above me; his own cock tenting his towel.

His face changed. It became acutely old and at the same time helplessly young. "You wouldn't act this way if I were Jeff," he said. There was a sneer to his lips, or, rather, a smug know-it-all expression as if he understood more about me than I wished to admit about myself.

I wrapped the towel back around my waist, gathered up my shampoo and soap, and left the room without saying anything else to him, the fury and shame and indignation pounding in my ears as I made my way back down the hall to my dorm room. It was months later before I saw Neal again. I stayed up late that night studying and when I returned to the dormitory after my final the next afternoon, Neal had already left for the summer break. When fall arrived and Jeff and I had settled into our off-campus apartment, Neal reappeared, and what had happened between us was forgotten.

I paused at the keyboard of the computer; the cabin lay quiet under the darkness of the night. The smoky air of the room chilled my shoulders and I felt a draft swirling at my feet like a restless cat. For a moment I thought about getting up to find a blanket to drape over my legs as I sat and worked, but decided I did not want the distraction, and kept working at the computer. Around me the ghosts of my past swirled and danced in the darkness and the breeze of my imagination. My life was different now from those days in college. I had changed, made it different myself, even as I adapted to the arbitrary obstacles life threw into my path.

Was the truth really what I had experienced or was it the detached facts compiled by an impartial observer, such as a reporter for a newspaper? Facts that could be read by an impartial observer days, months, maybe years later, after the event, devoid of history and emotion? Or was the truth in the emotion? Was the true story in the history of the characters? I could never simply write, 'Jeff did not love me. Kyle died of AIDS. I forgot about Mitch. Brice died in the Towers.' No, there was much more to each of those moments in my life. The same goes for 'Neal shot Perry.' Did Neal's self-confidence shatter his own ability to determine what was right and wrong? Could his aggression have been a mask for his insecurity? Or was this a mystery that would never be solved?

Neal and I never spoke of the incident in the dormitory bathroom, but it had stirred something inside of me, nonetheless—a danger that I knew I had to accept and learn to control—a recognition that I was a gay man and it was now time to come to terms with it and find a way to make it a better part of myself and my future. Neal had led me into beginning a relationship with Jeff in the fall of my junior year; we were mentor and beginner, sometimes experimental and instructional, but it was always adventurous and thrilling for me—at least in that first six months when we could not part from each other's side. We drank, fucked, slept, studied, fucked, slept, studied, and fucked some more, dancing through a cycle that blended day and night together, Jeff's body into mine and mine into his. Of course, I learned how to be resentful and aware of my vulnerability, what it was like to be young and in love and experience for the first time a broken heart and a wounded soul. But that passion and glow I felt in Jeff's company those early months became the prototype of what I sought and settled for from other friends and lovers after him. And Neal's aggression, in fact, had been a great and unexpected gift—a catalyst into my becoming the gay man I was now, seated before the computer keyboard, thinking, moving myself to write. I knew I had to find a way now to express my thanks for it, in spite of the man that he had become.

From the kitchen I heard the clatter of nails on the linoleum floor and I looked to the doorway and saw the dark blocky shape of Inky's body and wobbly legs. He cocked his head, his ears flopping and swaying at his side, and I knew he must be trying to see into the darkness of the room and make sense of the glow of the computer screen. He took a few more tentative steps, stepping out of the kitchen and onto the bare hardwood flooring of the Great Room. I rose and watched him move forward, worried he would slip or collapse at any second, then walked toward him, meeting him when he reached the back of the black bear-skin rug.

Inky sat down on his hind legs and I joined him on the floor at the rug, patting him as he drew in deep breaths of air through his mouth. "Think how much we've been through, old man, to make it here after all these years," I whispered to him. "Look at how we've survived. Think of the joy we've got ahead of us."

Outside the cabin the night darkened, or at least my perception of it faded away. My eyes felt raw and reddened, as if I had been crying, and I thought about returning to Harley and the warmth of him and the bed. I knew at that moment I was in love with him. Deeply in love and pleased with it. But I knew I could not sleep or, rather, knew that I could not sleep restfully. Instead, I stood and drew the giant black rug by the teeth of that devilish bear and pulled Inky across the floor, the quiet flame of emotion willing me to write again, the truth more important to tell than what I could hide.

JAMESON CURRIER

Jameson Currier is the author of seven novels: *Where the Rainbow Ends; The Wolf at the Door; The Third Buddha; What Comes Around; The Forever Marathon, A Gathering Storm,* and *Based on a True Story*; four collections of short fiction: *Dancing on the Moon; Desire, Lust, Passion, Sex; Still Dancing: New and Selected Stories;* and *The Haunted Heart and Other Tales*; and a memoir: *Until My Heart Stops.* His short fiction has appeared in many literary magazines and Web sites, including *OutsiderInk, Velvet Mafia, Blithe House Quarterly, Absinthe Literary Review, Confrontation, Rainbow Curve, Christopher Street, Genre, Harrington Gay Men's Fiction Quarterly,* and the anthologies *Men on Men 5, Best American Gay Fiction 3, Certain Voices, Boyfriends from Hell, Men Seeking Men, Mammoth Book of New Gay Erotica, Best Gay Erotica, Best American Erotica, Best Gay Romance, Best Gay Stories, Circa 2000, Rebel Yell, I Do/I Don't, Where the Boys Are, Nine Hundred & Sixty-Nine, Wilde Stories, Unspeakable Horror, Art from Art,* and *Making Literature Matter.* His AIDS-themed short stories have also been translated into French by Anne-Laure Hubert and published as *Les Fantômes,* and he is the author of the documentary film, *Living Proof: HIV and the Pursuit of Happiness.* His reviews, essays, interviews, and articles on AIDS and gay culture have been published in many national and local publications, including *The Washington Post, The Los Angeles Times, Newsday, The Dallas*

Morning News, The St. Louis Post-Dispatch, The Minneapolis Star-Tribune, The Philadelphia Inquirer Magazine, Lambda Book Report, The Harvard Gay and Lesbian Review, Dallas Voice, The Washington Blade, Southern Voice, Metrosource, Bay Area Reporter, Frontiers, Ten Percent, The New York Native, The New York Blade, Out, and *Body Positive.* In 2010 he founded Chelsea Station Editions, an independent press devoted to gay literature, and the following year launched the literary magazine, *Chelsea Station,* which has published the work of more than two hundred writers. In 2013, he edited two original anthologies: *With: New Gay Fiction* and *Between: New Gay Poetry.* The press also serves as the home for Mr. Currier's own writings which now span a career of more than four decades. Books published by the press have been honored by the Lambda Literary Foundation, the American Library Association GLBTRT Roundtable, the Saints and Sinners Literary Festival, the Gaylactic Spectrum Awards Foundation, and the Rainbow Book Awards. Mr. Currier is a member of the Board of Directors of the Arch and Bruce Brown Foundation, a recipient of a fellowship from New York Foundation for the Arts, and has been a judge for many literary competitions. A native of the South, he currently resides in New York.